Sea Horse in the Sky

SEA HORSE
IN THE SKY

A Science Fiction Novel
by EDMUND COOPER

G. P. Putnam's Sons
New York

Sea Horse in the Sky

1

It looked like Resurrection Day.

Or some incongruously daylight nightmare—with a touch of Brueghel, a dash of Dali, and a *soupçon* of Peter Sellers. It made you want to laugh or scream or something. Presently people began to do both—or something. Because there is nothing more likely to disturb, disorientate, or discommode than not knowing where, how, why, or even who.

Russell Grahame was the first one out of his "coffin." He was lucky. He knew almost immediately that he was Russell Grahame, Member of Parliament for Middleport North in the county of Lancashire.

He knew who, but he didn't know where, how, or why. He didn't even know when. So clearly it was just a crazy dream, and presently he would be woken up by the sound of someone saying, "Please fasten your seat belts and extinguish all cigarettes. We shall be landing at London Airport in about ten minutes."

But he didn't waken up, because he was already awake and the nightmare was real.

The "coffin" he had just vacated appeared to be made of pale green plastic. It lay in the middle of the road at the end of a neat row of similar coffins, between the building labeled "Hotel" on one side and the building labeled "Supermarket" on the other. The road was about ten meters wide and a hundred meters long. At each end it disappeared into grass and shrubs. It was just a thin oasis of urbanization in a great green wilderness. A taxi was parked outside the hotel. A car was parked outside the supermarket.

But there were no people—apart from those emerging from the man-size green boxes.

A dark-skinned girl literally kicked the lid off her box, stood up, shrieked piercingly, and fainted. It was the signal for general pandemonium. A man and a woman, both white, were the next to emerge. They looked round wildly, saw each other, and almost fell together, gripping so tightly that it looked as if they would never let go.

Two men got out of adjacent boxes, bumped into each other, fell over, and almost immediately started fighting. And almost immediately stopped.

Three girls were laughing and crying, terrified but finding an odd security in their mutual terror.

Presently, sixteen people, having got out of sixteen boxes, were themselves making enough noise to wake the dead or, at least, to excite the attention of any occupants of the hotel or the supermarket. But if anyone was in residence in the hotel or shopping in the supermarket, he was sufficiently familiar with the mechanics of resurrection in the middle of the main and only street not to wish to investigate further.

No one came out.

The pandemonium went on and on, with people talking, shouting, gesticulating, or babbling incoherently. They seemed dazed, traumatized, as if they had been through one hell of a harrowing experience. Which, of course, they had. And it was still happening.

Russell Grahame, feeling oddly detached from the whole absurd carnival, ran his left hand mechanically and repeatedly through his hair in the characteristic manner that had earned him the sobriquet Brainstroker among his few friends in the House of Commons. After a time he became aware that his head wasn't quite the shape it used to be. There was a bump somewhere in the region of the cerebellum. It was a fairly large bump, neat, round, and with a suggestion of scar tissue on top of it. The hair that covered the bump was nowhere near as long as the rest of his hair.

Russell Grahame, M.P., licked his lips and suddenly felt very shaky indeed. He needed a drink. He needed a drink rather badly. Glancing at the hotel, he walked slowly and cautiously toward it. It would not do for a Member of Parliament—even one who had finally made up his mind to get out of that madhouse where mass euphoria was permanently topped up with abstract nouns—to fall flat on his face in the middle of the road.

The hotel foyer was empty—except for an assortment of baggage piled in a heap near the revolving doors. There was no one at the reception desk. He hit the bell three times, but no one came.

Then he saw on the wall the words "Cocktail Bar" and an arrow pointing down a short passage. He went to the cocktail bar. That was deserted also. After a moment's reflection, he went behind the bar and poured himself a very large whiskey.

He took a good long pull at the whiskey. Then with trembling fingers he felt for his cigarettes. The noise outside seemed to be subsiding a little. He felt the bump on the back of his head and took another good swallow of whiskey. He began to feel a bit better.

Somebody else was hitting the bell at the reception desk. He was in no mood to go and enlighten them. Let them come to him.

They did. Or, rather, one did. The rest found their way later.

The newcomer was a man between twenty-five and thirty—tall, blond, blue-eyed, and rather good-looking in an extroverted, Continental sort of way. Grahame was immediately conscious of feeling anciently forty and very English.

"A large vodka, and what the hell has happened to the service?" demanded the tall young man truculently.

Obediently, Grahame poured the vodka. "Cheers. There is no service."

"Then who are you?"

The Englishman eyed his whiskey seriously and took another mouthful. "Just one of the walking dead. My name in Russell Grahame." Then he felt impelled to add, "British. . . . And you?"

His companion opened his mouth, closed it, put down the glass of vodka on the bar with a shaking hand, and looked very confused.

"Take your time," said Grahame sympathetically. "That is something I have a notion we are not going to be short of. Something tells me we are going to have all the time in the world."

"Norstedt," announced the young man, with a curious element of doubt in his voice. "I am Tore Norstedt. . . . Swedish. . . . Pleased to meet you."

He held out his right hand. Grahame shook it formally.

"Well, now we know each other. Have another drink. I'm going to." He smiled. "I think it's on the house."

"Thank you. Yes." Norstedt also smiled. "I think perhaps the vodka treatment is indicated." Absently he felt the back of his head.

Grahame noted the gesture. "Don't worry," he said. "I have a bump, too. It appears to be all part of the operation."

Norstedt slammed his glass on the bar so that some of the vodka slopped over. "What operation? Where are we? What the devil is going on?"

"Take it easy. I'm in the dark, too. When we have drunk some of the shakes away, we'd better try to make some sense out of it. . . . Incidentally, you speak excellent English."

Norstedt shook his head. "Swedish. I speak Swedish—as you are doing."

Grahame shrugged. "Have it your own way. But for the record, I don't speak Swedish—well, not much." A thought suddenly struck him. "Arlanda!"

"Yes, Arlanda!" repeated Norstedt excitedly. "That's it!" A piece of the jigsaw was falling into place.

"Arlanda Airport," went on Grahame. "The afternoon jet from Stockholm to London . . . That is where I saw you—at the airport. You were right ahead of me. You—you had excess baggage. Ten kronor . . . I wondered if I had enough money left to pay for mine."

"I remember! I remember!" Norstedt was almost shouting. "I couldn't find a taxi. I thought I was going to miss the plane."

"I have been watching your lips," said Grahame with a tightness in his voice. "By God, you are speaking Swedish! But the words I hear are English."

"I have been watching yours, also," observed Norstedt. "The—the shapes are not Swedish, but the sounds are."

While they exchanged these intriguing discoveries, Grahame had noted that the bell at the reception desk was being rung repeatedly, that voices were being raised in the foyer, and that those same voices were now getting louder as their owners came toward the cocktail bar.

"All roads lead to Rome," he observed grimly. "It seems, friend Norstedt, that we are about to have a rather interesting session."

2

It was, indeed, an interesting session. Also a baffling and bewildering one.

Russell Grahame elected to remain behind the bar. He made a very efficient bartender. Certainly, he reflected bitterly, he was better at mixing drinks than politics. Perhaps he should have taken a vocational aptitude test a quarter of a century ago. Then perhaps he might have wound up as a first-class barman in a five-star hotel instead of a third-rate politician, ground to a fine smoothness between the stones of a moribund two-party system. He had resigned from the Parliamentary Labour Party just before they were about to boot him out. With the same excellent sense of timing, he had decided while on holiday in Sweden to resign his seat when he got back.

If he got back . . . For factors were emerging that seemed to make the prospect somewhat remote. . . .

Still, for a while he did not have much time for thinking. He was too busy attending to the needs of his companions in adversity. Nobody questioned his right to control the bar. In fact, the general consensus seemed to be that he was a damn fine barman. Which was something. And with his own consumption of whiskey, his regret at never having taken an aptitude test increased.

Practically everyone was drinking spirits of one kind or another. Somehow spirits seemed to be appropriate to the occasion.

All sixteen people were now in the bar, having left their

crazy coffins in the middle of the crazy road in the crazy
ghost town that was the center of the crazy noncosmos
into which they had been thrust.

Introductions had been made, chaotically, spasmodically,
and whenever people managed to remember their own
names. The last person to rediscover identity was a slender,
decorative West Indian girl, improbably named Selene
Bergere. Her deliciously chocolate-colored limbs fell in a
graceful heap as she remembered this interesting fact while
disposing of a pretty powerful rum Coke.

She looked to be the youngest of the party, and she had
been the last to remember. Russell, glancing at the others,
judged that he was probably the oldest in the group. And
he had evidently been the first to remember. He wondered if these facts were significant.

Certainly it was a time for speculation.

Wild speculation . . .

However, before he lost himself entirely in a welter of
fantasy, or got drunk, or both, he decided to review the
facts that had so far emerged.

Fact one: There were sixteen people in the same predicament. Eight males and eight females. The sex balance was
probably no accident.

Fact two: Nobody knew why, how, where, or when.
Everyone's watch had stopped, including a battery-
powered model that was supposed—so its Russian owner
said in perfect English, Swedish, or what-have-you—to
keep going for a year.

Fact three: Everybody had bumps and scar tissue on the
backs of their heads. And, bearing in mind the international
composition of the party, everyone was able to speak perfect English, Swedish, French, Hindu, and Russian while
still apparently talking in their own native tongues.

Fact four: Everyone had been on the same jet from

Arlanda, Stockholm, to Heathrow, London. Although it had taken some time and some assistance before the younger members of the group were able to recollect this.

Fact five: Everybody's luggage was piled in the hotel foyer—something which Russell Grahame himself had failed to notice—being too intent, he supposed, on finding the bar. He had noticed the pile of luggage, certainly, but he had not connected it with himself or his fellow displaced persons.

Fact six: The town was not a town. Not even a village. It was just a hotel, a supermarket, and a few small buildings on either side of a strip of road that ran from nowhere to nowhere. It was more like a film set. And that presented a whole range of possibilities—from joke TV spectaculars up and down.

Fact seven: There were no people. Apart from sixteen prepackaged, untouched-by-human-hands humans, there were no people. Significant in the extreme, and a bit anxiety-making.

Fact eight: It was all real. None of your solipsistic finessing. It was all bloody horribly real.

"I have eight facts," announced Grahame to a man who had just stepped up to the bar with a trayful of glasses.

"I'm jolly happy for you, old boy," said Mohan das Gupta, age twenty-eight, Indian oil company executive. "How about sticking them in the icebox for a moment while you supply one lager and lime, one gin and lemon, one large brandy, and a Bloody Mary?"

"Furthermore, there are various conclusions to be drawn."

"Draw them by all means. But don't be too miserly with the brandy."

Obediently, Grahame supplied the drinks—but with an immense feeling of frustration. Everybody seemed to be talking their heads off—doubtless propounding all kinds of weird theories about what had happened and why. But the activity, the inquest, was uncoordinated. It lacked discipline and cohesion. In short, it wasn't going to get any bloody place.

Enter Russell Grahame, M.P., whose constituency meetings had been models of mediocrity and examples of ineffectuality that had constantly astounded the party workers of Middleport North. But hell, somebody had to do something.

"Ladies and gentlemen," he began in a loud voice. "Ladies and gentlemen, may I have your attention for a few minutes?"

"Why?" Somebody was already fairly drunk. "Don't you have enough with your own?"

"Because," explained Grahame patiently, "I dislike being part of a dream that is not a dream, because it's giving me a headache, and because I would like to get back to London sometime—if it is at all possible."

"Seconded," said a male, very British voice.

Faces turned toward Grahame expectantly, and he launched into his little speech. "I do not have to dwell on our method of arrival. We will all, I think, carry that little memory with us for some time. Nor do I have to labor the point—and humorous remarks will be appreciated later—that something decidedly peculiar has been done to all our heads. We have no time reference, none of us has any recollection of what happened on the flight from Stockholm to London, and I believe that none of us has the slightest idea where we are."

"South America," suggested somebody.

"Hollywood," countered somebody else.

"Please." Grahame held up his hand. "What I mean is that we do not have any evidence of where we are. There will probably be an embarrassment of theories, and we can discuss these at our leisure. But the only real evidence we have is evidence of the absurd. We came in what I can only describe as coffins, we find ourselves in a town that is demonstrably not a town, we are taking drinks in a deserted hotel, and we all appear to have received the gift of tongues. Now it seems to me that whoever—or whatever—has arranged this interesting situation has done so for a serious purpose. Further, since our luggage has been brought also, I do not think we can assume that our stay is intended to be a brief one."

"Come to the point, old sport," called the easily identifiable Mohan das Gupta.

"The point is," returned Grahame emphatically, "that we bloody well have to organize. Otherwise we may find that we are spending valuable time wringing our hands and crying into our gin and tonics."

"Excuse, please. What are you suggesting?" The speaker was a striking rather than beautiful dark-haired woman of perhaps thirty-five.

Grahame looked at her appreciatively. "Before we go any further, it may be a good idea if we identify ourselves so that afterward we shall know who has been advocating what. I am Russell Grahame, Member of Parliament . . . British, of course. . . . And you, madam?"

"Anna Markova. Journalist . . . Russian. . . . What are your politics, Mr. Grahame?"

"Do they matter?"

"They might."

"Very well. I am a socialist—of a kind."

Anna Markova shrugged. "It could be worse." Somebody clapped.

"Well, in answer to your question, Miss Markova, I think we should split into groups. I think that one group should explore the hotel and allocate accommodation—which I am betting will be needed. I think another group should explore our environs—the town and the immediate area surrounding it. I think a third group should endeavor to secure food supplies. And I think a fourth group ought to try to make some sense out of our predicament, besides helping with the efforts of the rest."

A tall slender man of about Grahame's own age—or perhaps a little younger—stood up. "I am Robert Hyman, civil servant, British. I think there is a great deal of sense in what Mr. Grahame says."

Another man spoke. He was blond and heavily built. "Gunnar Rudefors, teacher, Swedish. . . . Mr. Grahame is right. We must do something."

A girl spoke. She looked about nineteen, and she was sharing a table with two other girls. She was very nervous, and she could hardly be heard. "My name is Andrea Small. I'm a British student. Honestly, I'm just plain scared. Scared stiff. So are my friends. . . . We need somebody to tell us what to do."

"I'll go along with that—as I imagine most of us will." A large sandy-haired man was speaking. An attractively plump blond woman was sitting by his side. He went on: "My name is Paul Redman. I am an American literary agent." He glanced at his companion. "This is my wife, Marion. Since Mr. Grahame is the first of us to try to get something constructive off the ground, we feel that to begin with, at least, he should direct operations."

Tore Norstedt raised his glass to Grahame. "I think, sir, you have talked yourself into it." He glanced at the others. "Oh, I am Tore Norstedt, ship's radio officer. Swedish."

Grahame drank some more whiskey. "Before I confess that I may be foolish enough to accept the responsibility, does anyone object? Or alternatively, does anyone suggest another name?"

There was a silence.

Grahame smiled. "Very well, then. On your own heads be it. . . . But it is my experience that one cannot get things done if there is too much argument. Therefore I would like to introduce simple safeguards for me and all of you. One: I must have absolute authority. Two: If four people or more challenge that authority, someone else can take over. . . . May we have a show of hands?"

It was, thought Grahame as he surveyed his companions, the first and only time he had ever received a unanimous vote.

The bombshell came a few moments later.

A rather small, ineffectual-looking man stood up. "My name is John Howard, and I am a British teacher." He indicated the woman who sat next to him, nervously playing with her whiskey and water. "This is my wife, Mary. We both teach physics, and I think we have noticed something that may have escaped the rest of you." He hesitated. "It's rather startling. . . . Perhaps it is something I should discuss with Mr. Grahame privately."

Grahame shook his head. "I am not in favor of secrecy, Mr. Howard. I think I follow your reasoning. What you have to say may be alarming. But our predicament is already alarming, and I think we are all entitled to any information that can be obtained. So you had better tell us."

John Howard smiled apologetically. "It's rather negative, I'm afraid. . . . When you began to talk to us, someone suggested lightheartedly that we might be in South America or Hollywood. Regretfully, I'm afraid we must rule both those possibilities out."

"You know where we are, then?" asked Grahame hopefully.

"No. I only know where we are not."

"Which is?"

"We are not on Earth," said Howard sadly.

His disclosure was greeted with complete silence. All faces turned toward him.

Grahame licked his lips. "How do you know that?"

"I jumped—when we got out of the—er—boxes. I jumped. Inadvertently at first. Then, when I'd pulled myself together, I experimented." He grinned. "So did Mary, when she stopped crying."

"You jumped?" repeated Grahame, uncomprehendingly.

"Yes. I'm surprised you haven't noticed it already. You should have felt it. We are at less than one G. The gravity force on this planet seems to be about two-thirds that of Earth. . . . Test it if you like—but be careful you don't bang your head on the ceiling."

Solemnly, half a dozen people began to test jump. They soared three, four, five, and six feet into the air. They seemed to come down rather slowly.

Faces became white and strained. Nobody fainted. But one man and three women began to cry.

Russell Grahame poured himself a large whiskey, and decided that he had better begin talking again.

Very fast.

3

The rest of the afternoon—for they were able to determine that it was indeed afternoon by the position and movement of the sun—was a chiaroscuro of dramatic tension and sheer absurdity. The sun itself, though no one could look at it directly, seemed no different from the sun they had been accustomed to all their lives. Except that it appeared to move a little more rapidly down the sky.

Everyone had started their watches going again—apart from the electric one, which needed a new battery—and rough calculations indicated that this alien day would be about twenty Earth hours long.

Before Grahame organized his groups and tried to create some semblance of order out of chaos, he took a roll call of what he described with grim humor as his foreign legion. For the time being, he simply wrote down their names, ages, nationalities, and occupations so that he would have some rough idea of who to assign to do what. Later he could get more details and perhaps discover any useful aptitudes.

But for the present, he realized, he simply needed to get them all doing something quickly—if only to generate the illusion, however brief it might be, that they were not entirely helpless in this utterly bizarre situation.

No one could remember how many people had been on the jet from Stockholm to London, but the entire complement would certainly have been much more than sixteen. There would be time later to wonder what had happened to the pilots, the stewards, and the rest. For the moment it was wiser to concentrate on endeavoring to assess their present position and to make it as secure as possible under such abnormal circumstances.

The British contingent amounted to exactly half of Grahame's foreign legion. This, he reflected, would not be an unusual ratio on a flight from Stockholm to London toward the end of the tourist season.

He had meticulously recorded his own name at the head of his list and had followed it with the rest of the British displaced persons. After them came two Americans, two Swedes, an Indian, a Russian, a Frenchwoman, and a West Indian girl.

He studied the list carefully before forming his groups. It read:

Russell Grahame, 39, British, Member of Parliament

Robert Hyman, 39, British, civil servant

Andrew Payne, 28, British, television actor

⎧John Howard, 31, British, teacher
⎩Mary Howard, 27, British, teacher

Janice Blake, 20, British, domestic science student

Andrea Small, 20, British, domestic science student

Marina Jessop, 20, British, domestic science student

⎧Paul Redman, 40, American, literary agent
⎩Marion Redman, 32, American, no profession

Gunnar Rudefors, 35, Swedish, teacher

Tore Norstedt, 25, Swedish, ship's radio officer

Mohan das Gupta, 28, Indian, public relations officer (oil company)

Anna Markova, 33, Russian, fashion journalist
Simone Michel, 23, French, artist
Selene Bergere, 21, West Indian, model

The teaching profession was well represented, Grahame noted as he scanned the list, but that was not unusual. These days teachers seemed to do quite a bit of traveling, one way or another.

He sighed. It would have been more useful to have a doctor, a scientist of some kind, and perhaps one or two beefy general laborers than such people as the television actor, the literary agent, the public relations officer, and the sprinkling of career girls. One thing was clear: Whoever or whatever had staged the abduction, transference, capture—no single word would ever adequately describe it —he, she, it, or they had no thought of making a balanced party. Apart from the sex ratio. And that in itself was very intriguing. . . .

However, the implications could be contemplated later. For the moment, there were far more important matters to deal with.

He split his party up into four groups of four, according to his original suggestion. The general staff, which he also unsmilingly defined as a reserve task force, consisted of himself, Gunnar Rudefors, and Paul and Marion Redman. Two of the remaining groups were composed of two men and two women—they were the exploration groups—and the fourth group, whose primary duty was to secure a food supply, consisted of the Swedish radio officer and the three British girl students.

The general staff established itself in the cocktail bar. The others went about their business.

Presently interesting reports began to trickle back.

First and most important was that there was no sign of any living creatures within a radius of about one kilometer. The town consisted of nothing but the hotel, the supermarket, a strip of road, and a few small buildings that were equipped as simple workshops. The road itself began in wild grassland that might adequately be described as savanna, and it simply ended in savanna, also. The taxi that was parked outside the hotel was, apparently, a Mercedes. It did not have a battery or an engine. The car that was parked outside the supermarket was a Saab. That too had neither a battery nor an engine.

The supermarket was well stocked with food. Tore Norstedt and his three by now adoring girl assistants loaded large quantities of food into the trolleys that had been thoughtfully provided and wheeled them across the road to the hotel.

Meanwhile, two of the reserve task force—Gunnar Rudefors and Paul Redman—had removed the green plastic coffins and stacked them neatly behind one of the sheds. They had inspected the coffins thoroughly. The plastic, though light, was very hard and could not be scratched with a tough steel penknife. The interiors were lined with a spongy material which could be cut with a knife. Beyond these two facts they discovered little.

The hotel itself had twenty bedrooms, ten double and ten single. It also had a fully equipped kitchen, complete with refrigerator and dishwashing machine. And it had running hot and cold water in all rooms. And electric lighting that worked. It was, in fact, typical of a small but comfortable hotel that might have been found anywhere in Europe.

The electric lighting and running water provided Grahame with ideas to be followed up later. Eventually, he decided—if there were no distractions, visitations, or interruptions–it would be interesting to trace the plumbing and wiring back to source. Somebody or something was evidently taking a lot of trouble to ensure that sixteen displaced terrestrials should have a home from home.

Sunset came abruptly and dramatically–as it does on Earth in tropical and equatorial regions–and everyone gathered in the cocktail bar to make his report.

As it seemed pretty obvious that they had no choice but to spend the night–and quite possibly a long succession of nights–in the hotel, Grahame asked Anna Markova, who seemed a very capable woman, to allocate rooms. The three domestic science students were dispatched to the kitchen to put their theory into practice. And presently the entire complement sat down in the hotel dining room to a meal that would not have disgraced the Savoy–apart from the fact that all the food was processed.

At the coffee and brandy stage Grahame decided to hold an inquest on the entire sequence of events and threw the sixty-four-thousand-dollar/kronor/pound/rupee/franc ruble question down for discussion.

The most immediate and popular theory–born, no doubt, of cheap television and film productions and a multitude of cosmic strips–was that the group had been captured by Martians, Venusians, or some such solar race who had somehow descended from their flying saucers on the jet from Arlanda to Heathrow and had taken their hostages before destroying the aircraft.

John Howard, the British teacher, was the first to hit this notion on the head. He went to the dining room's French window, opened it, and stepped on to the balcony. It was a clear, cool night. He invited the rest of the company to join him.

The stars they saw in the sky were not of the constellations with which they had been familiar at home. Nor were they even of the constellations of the southern hemisphere. They were just alien stars in an alien sky. Bright, icy, remote. And terrible in their strangeness.

Acutely aware of the mood of anxiety, loneliness, and despair among his companions, Grahame hurriedly shepherded them back indoors. They sat gloomily at the dining tables and sipped their coffee. Conversation became frozen. Nobody was eager to discuss the awesome and awful possibilities that now presented themselves.

There was as yet no way of accurately defining time or the length of the night. But it was fairly obvious that everyone was tired out—two of the girl students actually fell asleep where they sat—with effort, with fear, with despair, and with thinking.

Too much had happened. Too many nightmarish possibilities had presented themselves for the human brain to cope with them. Everyone needed to rest.

But Grahame was determined that not everyone should rest—at least, not all at once. From the eight men he appointed night patrols, each consisting of two men who would be on duty for one hour. It would be their task to watch for intruders and to see that no one was harmed. As a further precaution, all bedroom doors were to be left wide open.

There were no strange incidents during the night—apart from occasional fits of weeping and subdued hysterics, indulged in almost as much—but much more discreetly—by the men as by the women.

But when morning came and a small exploration party went out of the hotel to check that things were still normal, they made a very interesting discovery.

The stack of coffins had disappeared.

4

There were other interesting discoveries made during the course of the second day.

Tore Norstedt, the young Swedish radio officer, was the first to find out that they were probably being watched. He had made the discovery shortly after he had gone off patrol duty and was lying on his bed in the dark, trying to will himself to sleep. He had noticed four tiny greenish points, palely glowing in the corners of his room where the ceiling met the walls.

He had switched on the bedside lamp—ordinary Earth-type with an ordinary sixty-watt bulb—and had explored further. In the light the greenish glow had disappeared; but set in the angle of walls and ceiling—and unnoticeable to any casual investigation—he discovered four lenses, one in each corner of the room. The lenses were hardly larger than match heads. But undoubtedly they were lenses. He wondered whether to chip the surface of the wall away and expose more of the equipment. Then, sensibly, he thought better of it.

He told Grahame of his investigation when they met for an early breakfast. A search revealed that there were similar lenses in every room and even in the corridors. The fact disturbed Grahame a great deal; and he asked Norstedt for the time being to say nothing to the other members of the group. Their situation was bad enough already without adding to it the burden of total loss of privacy.

Tore Norstedt wanted to tear out some of the equipment

and examine it and then perhaps destroy it; but Grahame restrained him. His political acumen provided what seemed like a sensible solution. When everybody had left his room, Norstedt would go around and stick small patches of paper over the lenses. But elsewhere in the hotel the lenses were to remain untouched.

Thus, reasoned Grahame, the watchers should be able to infer that their specimens, while not objecting in principle to observation, felt that they were entitled to some degree of privacy.

Immediately after breakfast he organized a more thorough investigation of their surroundings than had been possible or even desirable on the day of their arrival. This time the exploration group was composed solely of men, under the command of John Howard, the British teacher, who had already proved himself to be an observant and level-headed person.

Their instructions were simple. They were to march due north for one hour—north having been determined from the fact that the direction in which the sun rose was designated east—and then turn around and come back again. If they discovered any high ground, they were to use it to obtain a general view. But they were to avoid, if possible, all contact with any indigenous animal life; and short of being attacked and having to defend themselves, they were to do nothing that could possibly be interpreted as hostile action.

The question of self-defense was a thorny one. Grahame was loath to send men off on a possibly hazardous expedition without any means of protection. A search of the still unattended supermarket across the street revealed two interesting facts. The first was that the supplies that had been removed from it the day before had now been replenished. And the other was that it contained a small hardware section—which had apparently been overlooked the day before.

From the hardware section the four explorers took knives and small hatchets. As the day had already grown warm and the sun shone down through a cloudless sky, they had stripped down to light clothing. With shirt sleeves rolled up, knives stuck in their belts, and hatchets in their hands, they looked a formidable bunch of brigands.

Everyone turned out of the hotel to see them off on their journey into the interior. As they walked down the road that led to nowhere, brandishing their makeshift weapons and trying not to appear too self-conscious, they became most acutely aware of the absurdity of the situation. Even Grahame, who was beginning to feel that he had all the cares in this alien world upon his shoulders, could not help laughing. The expedition looked vaguely like a scene from the rehearsal of some comic opera.

They returned in exactly two hours and ten minutes.

All of them were safe. None of them had been in any kind of jeopardy.

But their report did nothing at all to alleviate the general mood of acute anxiety and insecurity.

First of all, John Howard reported on what all of them agreed they had seen. He estimated that they had traveled about eight kilometers over a plain that, apart from strange shrubs, small flowers, extremely large fernlike plants, and patches of surprisingly tough and very tall grasses, was fairly featureless. They had discovered a river, and in the middle distance they had seen a range of moderately high hills. But the party as a whole had not had any direct encounter with any animal life of any kind.

However, there were two minority reports.

One was by Paul Redman, the American literary agent. He said that as they had threaded their way between several clumps of grasses that were more than half as high again as an average man's height, he had stopped to wipe the sweat from his forehead. And he had gazed up at the sky.

Momentarily, he claimed, he had witnessed the passing of a brilliant and dazzling group of winged creatures. They had what looked like long golden hair, he said, and tiny faces that seemed almost human. And the only way he could adequately describe them was to say that they looked oddly like fairies.

The other report came from Gunnar Rudefors, the Swedish teacher.

The four men had traveled in single file, each man about half a dozen paces behind the one in front. Bearing in mind that they knew nothing at all of the country they were exploring, they had agreed that this was probably the safest way to move. As the lead position was obviously the most hazardous, each of them took turns at it.

Gunnar Rudefors took his turn when they were nearing their time limit and would shortly have to turn back. Being eager to make the most of the expedition, he had walked quickly and had pressed farther ahead of the others than he should have done.

Thus it was that he emerged from a long patch of tall ferns to catch a glimpse of what he insisted was a medieval knight in bright and curiously designed armor about twenty paces ahead.

Neither ridicule nor cross-questioning would shake Gunnar Rudefors from his description.

The knight wore something like a visor, so that his face was mostly hidden.

He also carried a weapon that might have been a kind of lance or sword.

He also sat astride an animal with large branched antlers, smaller than a horse but larger than a deer.

He and Gunnar Rudefors confronted each other for a long moment. Then the knight uttered a muffled word that sounded something like "Avaunt!" He swung his steed around by simply pulling on one of the antlers and cantered off into a group of trees.

By the time the rest caught up with the spellbound Swede, the knight had disappeared. John Howard, second in file, admitted that he heard something that might have been hoofbeats and a cry that could easily have come from Rudefors himself. But he saw nothing.

When Grahame had heard the account of the exploration jaunt, he realized that he needed a drink. A pretty large whiskey. Very badly.

He was not the only one.

5

Although no contact was established with the persons or creatures responsible for the abduction of sixteen passengers on the Stockholm-London flight, several interesting things happened during the next few days—two of them tragic. The first tragedy was the suicide of Marina Jessop, British student, age twenty. It took place on the evening of the day on which Paul Redman saw fairies and Gunnar Rudefors saw a medieval knight.

That evening after dinner Russell Grahame, M.P., officer commanding the extraterrestrial legion, reviewed the course of events and gave his interim interpretation. He tried to keep his speech—and it was a speech—as formal and as matter-of-fact as possible, bearing in mind the state of high emotional tension that already existed and would doubtless continue to exist until further notice.

"Ladies and gentlemen," he began, looking sadly at his small and strained audience, "I have been thinking a lot—as you all have—about what has happened to us. And despite the nightmarish absurdity of our plight and the tantalizing lack of information, I feel that for my own peace of mind (joke!) I must try to make some sense out of it. No doubt my interpretation is entirely wrong; but, for what it is worth, I give it to you. If, after I have spoken, anyone would care to submit a more valid explanation, I would be delighted to hear it. Meanwhile, here goes."

He paused.

"I am assuming that what has been done to us has been

done for serious and not frivolous reasons. So far as can be ascertained, we have all been abducted from an international jet flight, we have all been subjected to some kind of operation, and we now find ourselves on a strange world that must be an unimaginable distance from Earth. It seems to me that the entire operation—outrageous as it is—could only have been carried out by people or creatures with a science and a technology as much in advance of ours as ours is in advance of the Stone Age." He paused again, noted the misery on all faces, and added facetiously, "I refer, of course, to the terrestrial Stone Age. This planet, if we are to believe Mr. Redman, might well have a more picturesque prehistory."

He was hoping for at least a smile, but he did not get one.

He went on hurriedly. "The effort and the resources that must have been put into this project defy our twentieth-century minds. Colossal is a word that is not big enough. Therefore I submit, ladies and gentlemen, that we must have been brought here for a very serious purpose indeed. And I think that purpose is to find out what we of Earth—" he was oddly conscious of pronouncing the capital letter— "are like. Whether we shall ultimately be returned or not, I cannot possibly guess. But I am convinced that while we are here, our welfare wll be considered."

"What about the fairies?" asked someone.

"What about the knight?" asked someone else.

Grahame shrugged. "There is so much that cannot yet be answered. So much that may never be answered. One can only do one's best and guess. . . . And I am guessing, ladies and gentlemen, that we are regarded as zoological specimens. If there really are fairies and knights in existence, then I submit that they are probably collected specimens also. I have not the slightest idea where they may

The letter she wrote was addressed to Grahame personally.

Dear Mr. Grahame,

I am letting you down, and I am sorry. I am such a coward that I can't bear any more of this. Andrea and Janice will tell you that I have always been a timid person. I am afraid of darkness. I am even afraid of shadows. What has happened to us is the biggest shadow I have ever seen. It terrifies me so much that I can no longer go on pretending to be normal.

You must forgive me. You really must. Three days ago I was on my way home to my family after a lovely holiday in Sweden. I was even looking forward to the new term at college. But I know—as you must know—that none of us will ever get home. The thought petrifies me. I can't be a heroine. I haven't the strength to be a prisoner far from all that I love. And I should hate to go crazy and give you all a lot of trouble. So please understand and please forgive me. If you ever do get back, talk to my parents. They live at 71 Eden Street, Stockport, Cheshire. Please tell them I had an accident. I have a cat called Snowy, but I don't suppose you can tell him I had an accident.

Believe me when I say I would be no good to you or anyone.

Yours sincerely,
Marina Jessop

Grahame cried when he read the letter. He waited until he was alone, and then he cried. Marina Jessop had had a white—terribly white—face, he remembered. She had had

have come from. They may even be indigenous
planet. But clearly they or their kind cannot have
responsible for our predicament.

"It seems to me that there are two immediate necess
We must endeavor to find out as much as possible ab
the world to which we have been brought, and—short
antagonizing them—we must do our best to establish dire
contact with the people who have brought us here. N
doubt, compared to them we may seem like idiots or—o₁
animals. But if their ethical progress bears any relation to
their technological progress, we should be able to persuade
them—perhaps after a suitable period of study—to send us
home."

The discussion that followed Grahame's speech was
generally abortive. No one could suggest a better or a more
credible explanation, and in fact they were all too traumatized to think clearly. Eventually in ones and twos they
went to bed.

Sexual liaisons were already evident, Grahame noted.
And although there were only four married people in the
group, it was perfectly clear that at least another four
people had already assumed temporary married status. He
did not regard this as a bad sign. If anybody could derive
any comfort from sex or companionship, good luck to him.
It would probably ensure that he would stay sane a little
longer.

Marina Jessop had a room of her own. Her two friends
shared a room and had suggested that she come in with
them. But Marina had always been a rather solitary
creature and placed a premium upon privacy.

She went up to her room and wrote a short letter. Then
she went to take a bath. She was not discovered until next
morning. A portable electric radiator—apparently deliberately pushed into her bath—had solved all her problems.

long straight black hair and a far look, and she had reminded him of someone out of a Hans Andersen story.

She was the first casualty. He wondered how many more
there would be.

But life—such as it was—had to go on. Marina was buried
before midday in a little patch of fairly clear ground behind the hotel and about fifty meters from it.

Anna Markova, a professed atheist with a beautiful
contralto voice, sang the twenty-third Psalm for her. And
Mohan das Gupta, by birth a Hindu, made her a cross.

And life went on.

In the afternoon Grahame called upon his companions to
produce an inventory of their possessions, excluding
clothes and toilet things. He thought it a good idea to find
out what resources were available.

For the most part the list consisted of the usual tourist
equipment—cameras, small souvenirs of Sweden such as
glass and steelware, and a sprinkling of transistor radios
and books. But there were also some very useful items,
including a compass—which demonstrated that the planet
possessed magnetic poles—a pair of binoculars, two very
good first-aid kits, an assortment of pills, and even a
couple of portable typewriters.

Partly in order to distract people from Marina's death
and partly because he thought it was necessary, Grahame
planned a relatively ambitious exploration project. This
time the exploration party was to travel south. It was to
set out at dawn on the following day and was to return by
dusk on the day after. In this way, Grahame calculated,
the party would be able to go south for a full day's march
—perhaps twenty-five or thirty kilometers—before camping
for the night and then returning.

The prospect of spending a night in the open was possibly hazardous, but some risks would clearly have to be

taken if they were to learn anything of value about their surroundings. He asked for volunteers for the project.

John Howard, who had led the previous expedition, volunteered. So did his wife. Gunnar Rudefors offered to go again, and the fourth volunteer was Simone Michel, the French girl.

At first Grahame was dubious about letting women participate in such an undertaking. But then he realized that old-fashioned prejudices and inhibitions were not going to be of much help. Besides, as Anna Markova pointed out, women had different but certainly not inferior endurance characteristics than men. And it might well be that their presence would prove a stabilizing influence. Certainly it would prevent the men from taking any unnecessary risks.

Accordingly, the volunteers were dispatched to rest themselves, while the rest of the party set about making the necessary preparations. Four people, including the two remaining British students, were detailed to manufacture a tent and ground sheet from bed linen and plastic raincoats. Robert Hyman, the civil servant, revealed a hidden but useful talent. He was an amateur archer of some prowess. He offered to make a couple of longbows and a dozen arrows and to instruct the men in their use.

Tore Norstedt was busy making a crude spark transmitter out of bits and pieces and a coil of insulated copper wire that he had discovered in one of the workshops. The spark transmitter would serve two useful functions. If the exploration party took transistor radios, it would enable one-way radio contact to be maintained. And there was also the possibility that it could be used to establish contact with those who were responsible for their situation or with any other group of human beings in a similar predicament.

At dawn the following day all was ready; and everyone turned out to wish the "deep" exploration party good luck. Tore Norstedt had his spark transmitter working and had devised a simple telegraph key. He had already tested transmission and was confident that he could make signals effectively for at least forty kilometers, using the hotel's supply of electricity converted into rippling direct current.

The only trouble was that no one in the exploration party could read Morse code. And as Norstedt could not use his spark transmitter for the delivery of plain language, a very simple system of signals had to be devised. SOS meant return with all speed. OK meant proceed as planned. Transmissions would take place every hour on the hour.

Grahame was disappointed that there was not the possibility of two-way transmission. But as Tore Norstedt pointed out, to make a portable spark transmitter with the equipment available would take quite a lot of time and testing.

On the whole, the expedition was reasonably well equipped. It had homemade spears, knives, hatchets, two bows, and a dozen arrows. It had a tent and packaged rations. And it had a compass, binoculars, and a camera.

Nevertheless, Grahame waved it off with a heavy heart. The previous party had not gone far before two of its members had discovered what looked like fairies and a knight. This expedition was journeying several times farther into the interior. He did not really care to contemplate what news it might bring back—if, indeed, it managed to get back.

His fears were not unfounded.

At dusk the following day the party returned. Or, rather, three members returned.

Gunnar Rudefors, who had been leading the group on the last leg of the journey, had fallen into a concealed pit. He had been impaled on sharpened stakes.

6

Russell Grahame sat on his bed in his own room late at night, brooding upon the deaths of two of his companions in three days. He had brought a half bottle of whiskey up with him and was proceeding to demolish it systematically. Solitary drinking had never appealed to him before. It did not appeal to him now. He was leaning on the whiskey as a man with a broken leg might lean on a crutch.

At the rate he had been drinking it during the last few days, he told himself, he stood a fair chance of breaking all speed records for becoming an alcoholic. It was a good job the invisible replenishers kept topping up supplies. Though how they did it was a complete mystery. He had arranged for a night watch to be kept on the supermarket, but no one had detected any visitation. Yet every morning whatever had been taken out on the previous day was restored. It was a hell of a mystery. But then what was one bloody mystery among so many?

He felt desperately lonely. There were obvious reasons for that. Perhaps it would not have been so bad, though, if he had not been so damned egotistically public-spirited as to accept leadership and with it the concomitant of responsibility. People looked at him and asked him things as if he were supposed to know all the bleeding answers.

Hell, he didn't even know the right questions. A fine leader, indeed!

He poured himself some more whiskey.

Because he had accepted responsibility, he felt the loss

of the British girl and the young Swede all the more keenly. Salud, Marina! Salud, Gunnar! May your bones and spirits rest in peace on this alien world far from the green fields of Earth. . . .

He tried to concentrate on the information that the survivors of the second expedition had brought back with them. It was more alarming even than the minority reports from the first expedition. For on the second journey everyone agreed on what they had seen. And they had brought back instant photographs to prove it.

Apart from Gunnar's death, the most disquieting event on the second expedition had been the discovery of other human beings—the People of the River, as they were now being called.

Simone, the young French artist, had been the first to spot them. They might easily have been missed, because the party was about twenty kilometers from "home" and traveling on a course roughly parallel with the river, which was about two kilometers from them. Simone had chased after what she believed to be a large and gorgeous butterfly which she had evidently surprised as the party was traveling through heavily wooded country. The butterfly seemed to be moving rather slowly—almost, she suggested later, as if it were trying to lead her.

Perhaps it was. The party was already near the edge of the patch of forest, and the pursuit of the butterfly took her out into open country on a small rise, where she could look down slightly on the river. She promptly lost the butterfly. But luckily she was carrying the binoculars. Idly she used them to look at the river. What at first appeared to be a rough bridge turned out not to be a bridge when she focused carefully. Or, rather, it was a bridge of rough huts built upon piles. Smoke was coming through roof holes. The occupants of the huts were evidently at home.

Sensibly, the exploration party approached the small colony of river dwellings very cautiously indeed. They did not go nearer than half a kilometer, and they conducted their investigation with the aid of the binoculars.

The river people—and there were several of them on the near bank—looked rough and shaggy and seemed to be clothed in animal skins. They looked for all the world, said John Howard, like refugees from the Stone Age. They had axes and clubs, apparently with stone heads, and spears with stone blades. They also had what seemed to be hollowed log canoes.

Wisely, John Howard decided not to investigate more closely—in case of accidents. He thought it was more important to bring the information they had already discovered back to base. However, he spent some time studying not only the People of the River with his binoculars but also the surrounding terrain. In the distance, on the far side of the river, he found what he could only describe as a high, unmoving wall of fog or mist. It seemed to be five or six kilometers away, and he judged that it must be at least a couple of hundred meters high.

The party retreated to the forest to camp for the night, which they spent with two people watching and two people resting for hourly spells. They heard some rather disturbing sounds of wild animals but saw nothing. On the following day it was not until they were no more than seven or eight kilometers from home that Gunnar Rudefors fell into the pit.

It was not a very big pit. But it had been cunningly placed in a barely distinguishable track—perhaps the watering route of some herd creatures—that the party must have been subconsciously following. The sharpened stakes killed him almost instantly. They had been arranged so that they would achieve minimum damage.

Gunnar was doubly unlucky. Unlucky that he was leading at the time, and unlucky that he did not notice that the
patch of grass ahead of him was curiously brown. . . . .
    As he mulled over all that had happened since he had
stepped out of his coffin and entered the hotel, Russell
Grahame was acutely aware of his own inadequacy.
Leader, indeed! He was not fit to lead a troop of Boy
Scouts.
    If he had had any sense, he would have kept people so
busy that Marina would have been too tired to contemplate suicide. If he had had any sense, he would not have
allowed exploration parties to venture forth until they had
trained themselves very carefully. If he had had any
sense. . . .
    Leader, indeed! Decision maker, indeed! By God, now
was the time to jack it in before everybody got fed up and
deposed him.
    There was a knock at the door. It opened.
    "May I come in?"
    Anna Markova granted herself permission before he
could reply.
    "Hello, Anna."
    "Hello, Russell."
    Everyone was on first-name terms now. There was no
point in formality when you were stuck x light-years from
the nearest book on etiquette. And it was strange—very
strange—how, with the gift of tongues, nationality no longer
mattered.
    Anna glanced at the whiskey. "Do you like drinking
alone?"
    "No."
    She smiled. "Then you should offer me some."
    "I'm sorry. I didn't mean to be rude. . . . Can you

manage with a tooth glass, or shall I go down to the bar for another whiskey glass?"

"The tooth glass will do, thank you." She sat on his bed and bounced up and down a little. "This bed is more comfortable than mine, I think."

"Complain to the management," he suggested with the ghost of a smile. "Alternatively, I would be happy to change rooms with you."

She changed the subject abruptly. "You are full of sorrow, Russell. It is natural to mourn the dead, but one should not do it alone. And this," she glanced at the glass of whiskey he had given her, "this will not help as much as you hope."

"Amen," he said, raising his own glass.

"Amen," repeated Anna, drinking with him. "This is the first opportunity I have had of talking alone with you. I shall tell you what I think, and then you shall tell me what you think. Agreed?"

"Agreed."

"Well," she went on, "it seems obvious that we are in a kind of zoo. On Earth in the more modern zoos," her eyes twinkled, "or at least in modern Russian zoos we try to ensure that the animals have surroundings that are as natural as possible. I think our captors have done this for us. That is why we have been given a hotel to live in, why we are able to get what we need from a supermarket or store, and why there are cars on the street."

"The cars don't work."

"Naturally. There is nowhere for us to drive them. But our captors know that we are accustomed to these things, and so they have tried to make us feel at home."

"Their solicitude would be more appreciated if they would return us home," he remarked somberly.

"They will not do that," said Anna.

"Why not?"

"We are—or were—eight men and eight women."

"So?"

She regarded him with sad amusement. "The implication is obvious, Russell. We have been brought here to breed. . . . Do you not think so?"

He did not answer. Nor did he meet her gaze.

"I see you do think so. It is better to face facts, isn't it? We have been brought here to breed. And if that is so, it is most unlikely that we shall ever be returned to Earth."

Now he looked at her and was amazed by the calmness of her expression. "The thought does not terrify you?"

She shivered momentarily. "One must face it and accept it. Then life can go on. Life has to go on, Russell. What has happened is dreadful and wonderful. We cannot let it be pointless."

"What do you mean?"

"Only that we *shall* breed. There are married people in our group, and already other liaisons are developing." She laughed rather grimly. "I do not think you will find any supplies of contraceptives in our obliging supermarket, Russell."

Impulsively he took her hand and held it. "Has it occurred to you, Anna, that these people or creatures or whatever have just picked us up as biologists collect specimens? That we may simply be experimental material to them and that when the experiment is over . . ." He stopped.

"They will have no further use for the specimens?"

Russell nodded.

"That is possible," conceded Anna. "But I do not think it is probable. In any case, we must act as if it were not so. Otherwise—otherwise life would be unbearable."

"Is it not becoming so?"

"No."

He laughed. "I think you must have a very resilient personality."

"Perhaps. But it will only stay resilient if . . . Do you find me attractive, Russell?"

"I find you very attractive, Anna."

"Do you have a wife or a family in England?"

"No. I have been far too busy being a bad socialist to indulge in anything so—so creative."

She smiled. "Then you shall have your chance. I am a bad Communist but a very practical woman. I am not a virgin, and I have learned not to expect too much from men. . . . So I shall come and live with you, and we shall learn to keep each other warm. Sex might be enjoyable for us both, I think, but it must never become a duty. After all, there is something much more important—friendship. Don't you agree?"

He looked at her silently for a moment or two—with eyebrows raised. Then he said solemnly, "Anna Markova, I am slightly drunk, and you are a very remarkable woman."

"That is settled then. If we do not suit each other, the arrangement—not the friendship—can easily be ended."

Russell raised his glass. "God bless Karl Marx."

Anna stood up, raising her own glass, and announced, somewhat inscrutably, "The Queen." Then, having disposed of her whiskey, she went to collect her few possessions.

Suddenly Russell Grahame realized that his mood of depression had left him and that his confidence had returned. It took him a few moments to understand why.

Then he discovered that he was no longer lonely.

7

Extract from the diary of Robert Hyman:

This is the fifteenth night of our stay on a world which it amuses Russell to call Erewhon. I doubt if he has ever read Samuel Butler; but no matter. The name fits for obvious reasons. As far as the rest of the human race is concerned, we are indeed nowhere. Some of us will be missed and mourned greatly. One consolation is that I shall not. I was alone there, and I think I shall still be alone here. That is the privilege of being a homosexual without the courage of one's convictions.

For a while, I had hopes that Andrew—poor Andrew, the lean and languid star of that terrible television spy series— might be similarly afflicted/blessed. But no. Andrew, dear boy, is just effeminately masculine. And now God knows if he will ever be any use to anybody. He's quiet enough at the moment; and perhaps we shall shortly be able to take our homemade straitjacket off him. Certainly we can't hope to nurse him forever. I am beginning to think he would have been better off if he had made a good job of cutting his throat.

His babbling about great metal spiders has unnerved us all. From the few coherent phrases he has given us, it sounds as if he got up in the middle of the night to take a turn along the one short street in our little ghost town. He claims he saw these creatures heading for the supermarket with armfuls of groceries—though the two night guards saw and heard nothing. All that is really certain is that we found Andrew just before dawn, lying outside the hotel stiff as a board, eyes wide and staring. We finally got him literally to unbend. But at that stage he went deadly quiet and wouldn't say a word. The next thing we knew, he had locked himself in his bathroom and was sawing away with a razor blade, shouting his head off and making one hell of a mess.

I suppose it's a good thing that Marion Redman knows a little about nursing. He hadn't done any real damage, but it looked as if he might have bled to death. And now the poor boy does nothing but sit there in his bandages and straitjacket, rolling his eyes a little and muttering occasionally about metal spiders with packs of detergents and canned goods.

Still, there remains the question of how our supplies are replenished. We have guards, but nobody has ever seen anything except Andrew. John Howard has a theory that we have been conditioned not to see. Tore has an even wilder theory that our captors can "switch us off" whenever they wish. He claims they simply forgot to switch off Andrew.

However, we are still no nearer to solving any of the mysteries that surround us. Perhaps we are just not meant to solve them. . . .

Tonight I confessed. I don't know why. It seemed important. Perhaps because everyone seems to be pairing —or tripling—off. Tore Norstedt has taken both Janice and Andrea into his room. Nobody seems to care. Why should they? Mohan das Gupta is having a wild and tempestuous affair with Simone. She, apparently, wants to paint him, but he wants to make love all the time. And poor little Selene Bergere—what an impossible name—is wistfully and distantly lusting for our revered leader.

Meanwhile, John and Mary remain placidly devoted, and Paul and Marion only quarrel when they think they are alone.

I like Russell. Perhaps that is why I confessed. He is the first person apart from Sammy—and Sammy, poor sweet, died so long ago I can hardly remember his face—who ever knew.

I thought Russell might wonder why I didn't try to "comfort" one of the girls. Hell, no, I didn't! I just wanted to tell him. He didn't give a damn.

All he said was, "Robert, old boy, you are among friends. I only wish it was a bit easier for you."

I knew what he meant, of course. Still, loneliness is something I'm familiar with.

Apart from experiencing two deaths and one breakdown, and apart from reports of fairies, medieval knights, and savages, we are really no wiser now about our predicament than when we first arrived. The zoo theory is the most popular one. It is also the most reasonable one. But how tantalizing not to know who runs the zoo!

Anna is convinced they want us to breed. Being methodically Russian, she is not offended by the notion. In fact, she threatens to provide Russell with half a dozen sons—in the fullness of time.

We have done a bit more exploring, of course. Or, at least, we did before Andrew encountered his spiders. But it was only a bit because Russell has insisted that we all do it together. Safety in numbers, and all that. If the zoo keepers have an efficient observation system, they must laugh themselves silly when they see us go trailing off for "field exercises" armed with bows and arrows, spears, and homemade bludgeons.

Actually, I think Russell is less intent on exploring at this stage than on making us all a bit tougher and a bit more self-reliant. I think he is working up to something.

8

It was three o'clock in the afternoon, Standard Erewhon Time. The heat was oppressive. The days seemed to be getting longer and warmer; and with the strange and feathery seeds of tall grasses blowing in untidy heaps along the street, there was every indication that it was high summer.

Russell Grahame sat on the steps of the hotel, holding a photograph in his hand and idly watching the drifting seed pile up against the useless Mercedes and the equally useless Saab. He wondered how long it would be before both cars were snowed under. The seed blew in from the great green savanna in visible clouds. It had caused several people to have acute but brief attacks of hay fever; but apart from that it seemed harmless enough. At the rate it was coming in, the whole street would probably be two or three inches deep in it during the course of the next few days. Perhaps, thought Russell, he ought to get a task force tidying the old town up. But he was feeling listless, as everyone else was; and the time to sweep the seed away would be when it had stopped blowing in.

Russell was not alone. Andrew Payne, sans straitjacket but not sans bandages, was sitting beside him. So was the brown, childlike, and curiously ethereal Selene Bergere. Selene had confessed some time ago that her real name was Jojane Jones. But nobody thought of her as Jojane. The name Selene seemed to fit her like a glove.

Ever since he had tried to commit suicide, she had appointed herself Andrew's nurse. Now that he was almost back to normal, she still looked after him very carefully; and between the two of them there seemed to have developed a curiously touching brother and sister relationship.

Andrew's return to normal, after many days of sheer vacancy alternating with brief fits of hysteria, was greatly assisted by the photograph that Russell now held in his hand.

It was a flash photograph. The camera had been fixed in the supermarket, trained on the doorway and with its shutter operated by a simple trip string. Paul Redman had provided the equipment and rigged the camera up. Luckily, he had been traveling from Stockholm to London with two packs of film and a half a dozen flash bulbs still unused. Tore Norstedt had added a refinement to the operation by arranging for the trip string also to set off a homemade electric buzzer.

So it was possible to determine when the photograph had been taken. And it had been taken at about two-thirty in the morning.

It showed—with tantalizing lack of detail—the outline of a metallic spider carrying a crate of groceries, presumably to replenish stocks.

Thus was Andrew vindicated, the corroboration of his "vision" working like a therapeutic charm.

Russell glanced again at the photograph, for about the twentieth time. The body of the spider was no larger than a football, with a small inverted cup shape—possibly the sensing mechanism—set on top of the smooth sphere. It walked, apparently, on four multijointed legs and was also using four multijointed arms to support the box of groceries over its head/body. The entire machine—for clearly it was a machine—was no more than about a meter high.

"What do you make of it?" asked Andrew, gazing almost lovingly at the print that had helped to restore his sanity. "Do you think it has intelligence?"

"Possibly," conceded Russell. "But I am betting that it is more likely to be a remote-controlled robot. . . . Of course, our trouble is that we are conditioned by orthodox human concepts. For all we know, this little joker could be the lord of the planet, having perhaps superseded his biologically based creators. But I'm still betting he's a relatively simple robot—the long arm, if you like, of his shy, retiring masters."

Selene shuddered and moved closer to Andrew, who put his arm around her protectively and so gave Russell some inward amusement.

"I frighten easily, Mr. Russell," she said. Because he was the acknowledged leader of the group she always referred to Grahame as Mr. Russell, despite his protestation. "I frighten very easily. What if there are hordes of these things, all waiting just to pounce on us?"

Russell laughed. "If they were going to pounce, Selene, they would surely have pounced some time ago. Instead of which, as you must admit, we have been looked after—or, at least, our needs have been provided for—very well. Personally, I think their basic task is to look after us and to—" He stopped.

Mohan das Gupta had just come out of the supermarket. He ran across the street to them.

"No bloody cigarettes," announced Mohan.

"Well?"

"There were dozens of packs yesterday, but now there aren't any."

Grahame thought for a moment. "Are you sure nobody has been shopping before you?"

"It was my turn to bring the supplies over," said Mohan. He grinned. "Perhaps somebody is playing funny games."

"I doubt it," said Russell. "It's too hot for fun or games."

"Reprisals," said Andrew suddenly. "They are making reprisals."

"I beg your pardon?" For a moment Russell did not connect.

"The spiders—or whoever controls them—don't like curiosity," explained Andrew. "I saw one of them and I wound up as a temporary nut case, trying to carve myself. You can say I was scared out of my wits, of course—and I admit I was—but I can't help thinking that somehow somebody gave me a helping hand when I went around the bend. . . . Now we have managed to take a picture of one of them. They couldn't make the camera have fits, and maybe for some reason they did not want to destroy it, so they are trying to discourage us by withholding something they know we use in great quantities."

"An interesting theory," conceded Russell. "The evidence is merely circumstantial. . . . But—it could be so."

"Or perhaps it's more simple than that, old sport," suggested Mohan with a grin. "Maybe they have simply run out. Maybe the chaps back at base didn't count on us all becoming chain smokers." He shuddered comically. "Oh, evil day! It's the devil of a long jaunt to the nearest tobacconist's."

"Of course," said Russell slowly, "the way to test Andrew's notion is to set up the camera again and take another picture."

Mohan's eyes gleamed in his dark face. He threw up his hands in horror. "Not bloody likely! We can't risk them cutting off the gin."

Selene gripped Andrew's arm very tightly. "Look!" she said, pointing down the street. "Oh, my god! Oh, my god! What is it?"

A strange apparition seemed to have risen suddenly out of the bright green backcloth of the savanna. It began to walk or lurch almost drunkenly along the short strip of road toward them.

"Now I will believe almost anything," said Russell in a tight voice. "Gunnar was right. There are knights as well as fairies at the bottom of our garden."

9

The knight—if such he was—seemed to be in a very sorry condition. He wore only breast armor, which might have been made of bronze, and some kind of leather trousers and jerkin. If he had had a helmet or visor, he had lost it; and his steed—if any—was nowhere in sight.

His face, at first glance a curious blend of Mongol and Negro, had bloodstains upon it. His trousers and the patch of jerkin below his breast armor were ominously wet and red. Clearly he was suffering from multiple wounds. But he was still strong enough to carry a kind of sword in his right hand.

The small group on the steps of the hotel were temporarily frozen into immobility. The knight lurched on toward them. His eyes were wide and staring, but he seemed to be aware of nothing in his immediate vicinity, being perhaps preoccupied by things that none but he could see.

Even as he sat frozen, waiting, Grahame's mind was operating at lightning speed. Everything seemed to be reduced to slow motion, so that he was able to register the most minute details of the knight's appearance. He saw the holes punctured in the leather clothing, the bruises, the fragments of soil and grass that clung to clothing, armor, and face. He fancied he could see the blood pulsing out of hidden wounds—even that he could hear the beating of the man's tortured heart.

The knight staggered on toward the hotel. At every third

or fourth step he struck—or tried to strike—at an invisible enemy.

Presently, after half a century or ten seconds, Grahame pulled himself together, got up, and walked toward the strange being.

Suddenly his presence was noted. The knight stopped moving and swayed drunkenly upon his feet. With a tremendous effort he managed to focus upon Russell. What he saw, evidently, did nothing to inspire confidence. He tried to lift his sword, almost fell over, and tried hard again. He couldn't make it. With a muffled curse he stabbed the point of the sword against the road and leaned on his weapon as on a crutch.

He coughed painfully, then spat at Russell. Then, with a supreme effort of will, he managed to raise the sword.

"Avaunt," he said thickly, apparently in excellent English. "Begone, demon, hobgoblin, sprite, devil, warlock, spirit of evil. In the name of the white queen and the black, I command you. Return to the dark earth whence you came."

Russell did not move. Idiotically, he could think of only one thing to say: "Peace."

"Peace!" roared the warrior dreadfully. "Peace! You would mock me in my weakness! Then die, wretched one, knowing that Absu mes Marur is hard put, otherwise the blade would not grace thee."

The knight lunged. Russell stepped to one side. Even if he had not moved, the attack would never have been completed. For the stranger had evidently used up his last reserves of energy. Without a sound he fell flat on his face.

Russell turned him over very gently. Drained of color, the man's face was almost white. It seemed pathetically young.

10

Absu mes Marur, lord of sept Marur, gonfalonier of the western keeps, charioteer of the red spice caravans, holder of the royal falchion, and elected sire of the unknowns, lay unconscious for more than two days in one of the rooms of what it amused Mohan das Gupta to call the Erewhon Hilton. His wounds were grievous, but none by itself was fatal. If he had been a terrestrial, he would probably have died of trauma, infection, and loss of blood. But whatever else he was, Absu mes Marur was not a man of Earth; and, late in the afternoon of the third day, after the fever had worn off, he opened his eyes.

Marion Redman had stayed with him much of the time. She had cleaned his wounds, bathed his burning forehead, and had generally endeavored to make him as comfortable as possible. While this was going on, John Howard and Tore Norstedt had been dispatched north, south, east, and west in turn on short scouting trips to see if they could contact any of the stranger's companions. But they found no one. Grahame was unwilling to let them go more than three or four kilometers away for obvious reasons. If any of the knight's friends—or enemies—showed up of their own accord and chose to be truculent, there could be some rather serious problems.

Grahame was present in the room when Absu mes Marur returned to consciousness.

"Do not move," said Grahame evenly. "No one here wishes you any harm. You have been very near to death.

When you have rested and recovered yourself, we will—if you wish—escort you home. . . . That is, if we can discover where you live."

The man on the bed rolled his eyes and shuddered. He felt for his armor, but Marion had cut the harness to get it off him two days before. He felt for his sword, but that also had been removed.

Grahame sensed the man's unease at what he obviously considered to be his nakedness. With some wisdom he took the sword from a cupboard where it had been kept and laid it on the bed so that the knight could rest his hand on the hilt. He was rewarded with a look of gratitude.

"Whether you be man, ghost, or demon," said the knight quaintly, "I would hear the sound of your name, rank, and titles. Here before you, shamed in his own eyes, as in yours, lies Absu mes Marur, lord of sept Marur."

"How do you do," said Grahame carefully. "I am called Russell Grahame."

"Lord of your sept?"

"I do not understand."

Absu mes Marur was still very weak, and he was rapidly tiring himself out. But he was clearly determined to find out as much about his circumstances as possible.

"This woman," he said faintly. "She is your woman?"

"No, she is not."

The knight sighed. "Then I shall not speak with you. Bring to me the lord of your sept."

Marion got the message first. "He wants to know if you are our leader, Russell. Set the poor fellow's mind at rest before he pushes his temperature into overdrive."

"I am the chosen leader of my people," said Grahame. "I hope you can understand. We do not have a sept, as you call it, but I am the chief man, if you like, among my friends and companions."

Absu mes Marur smiled faintly. "You are the lord of your sept. Know that your metal will not be disgraced when I am able to lift my sword."

"I will not willingly fight you," said Grahame. "Now or ever."

"It is your duty."

"It is not my duty. My duty is to take you to your home when you are well enough to travel."

Again the knight shuddered. Then he attempted to pull himself together. "I am gonfalonier of the western keeps, charioteer of the red spice caravans, holder of the royal falchion, and elected sire of the unknowns," he announced with some pride. "Whoso dares to disgrace me may, in the end, need many squadrons of lances to preserve him."

"No one wishes to disgrace you," said Grahame patiently. "I and my companions wish only to help you. . . . We will fight if we must, but we wish to live in peace. We desire to be your friends. We desire also that you and your people should be our friends. Now rest, Absu mes Marur. No one will harm you."

The knight was breathing heavily, and sweat beaded on his forehead. "What is your rank?"

"I have no rank."

Absu mes Marur groaned.

"For Christ's sake, Russell!" exclaimed Marion. "Tell him something. The poor bastard is off his trolley with anxiety."

"My dear," said Grahame, "wasn't it Oscar Wilde who said we are separated by the barrier of a common language? He appears to speak English—though we know he can't, and his lips make different word shapes—so he has probably had something done to his head, like us. The trouble is, although we can communicate, his concepts are completely alien—medieval alien, I imagine."

"Your rank!" shouted Absu mes Marur desperately.

Russell shrugged. "Oh well, here goes." He turned to the knight. "I am Russell Grahame, Member of Parliament," he announced impressively. "Voice of the Queen's people, creator of the royal laws, holder of the 1939–45 star, and member of the Royal Automobile Club."

Absu mes Marur nodded eagerly and uncomprehendingly. "Then you are in truth lord of your sept?"

"So be it. I am lord of my sept. . . . But we belong to different worlds, you and I. Try to understand that. I and my people come from a world that is beyond the stars and on the far side of the sun. We were brought here in a way which—"

Absu mes Marur opened his eyes wide, uttered a piercing cry, and retreated once more to the merciful haven of unconsciousness.

11

It took several days before Absu mes Marur's wounds were sufficiently healed for him to be able to walk once more. During that time he and Russell Grahame learned a great deal about each other and about the quite different worlds from which each of them came. In this respect Grahame had the considerable advantage of having been reared in a technological and emotionally sophisticated society. He was able to grasp ideas and concepts that were far beyond the mind of one whose culture was roughly similar—as Grahame had surmised—to that of the European Dark Ages.

The one thing that continued to surprise Russell Grahame and his companions was that Absu was indisputably human. Familiar though he was with the beginnings of space exploration and the preparations for interplanetary travel that were already being carried out on Earth, Grahame had never given much thought to its breathtaking possibilities. He had imagined that such journeyings must of necessity be confined to the solar system, since the gaps between the stars were too vast to be spanned effectively by "conventional" modes of travel.

But he and his companions had received by their own experience dramatic confirmation that long star voyages were not only possible but could be accomplished with relative ease. However, because the terrestrials had been unconscious, presumably, during their abduction, there was no way of knowing the subjective time that had been needed to transport them to Erewhon. They could have been in their plastic coffins—possibly under some kind of suspended animation—for minutes or centuries. Perhaps one day their captors—if, indeed, they ever revealed themselves—might explain the mechanics as well as the purpose of the abduction. But for the time being, all was wild speculation.

It became clear, though, after some discussion, that the terrestrials were not alone in their bafflement or in their isolation from the world they had known. Absu mes Marur *and fifteen companions* had arrived on Erewhon in a similar fashion. The only difference was that they had not been taken from an airborne transport but from an earth-bound caravan consisting of merchants, warriors, women, and pack beasts transporting the precious red spice of the Kingdom of Ullos to the Upper and Lower Kingdoms of Gren Li.

That these kingdoms, as Absu described them, could not exist on any planet of the solar system, Grahame was absolutely certain. He knew enough about the solar system to realize that only Earth, the third planet, was naturally favorable to the evolution of human life.

Yet Absu mes Marur, whose planet of origin must therefore belong to an alien star, was undeniably human. On Earth he might have passed as the result of mixing African and Asian blood. But he was not of Earth, nor even of the Sun's family. Yet he was human. And, as time passed, Grahame began to entertain the equally baffling notion that Absu mes Marur and his kind would turn out to be genetically compatible with the men and women of Earth.

He thought grimly of Anna Markova's lighthearted threat that she would bear his children. If things did not go well in this fantastic situation that was developing—or, indeed, if things went too well—poor Anna and the other women in the group might find that they would be faced with the possibility of bearing—in every sense of the word—far more than they could at present imagine.

In the matter of his origin Absu was not a great deal of help. Despite his initial horror and humiliation—inspired, no doubt, by strange taboos or attitudes—he came to trust Grahame and even to accept his friendship.

"Let us talk, Absu," said Grahame one morning when the knight was well enough to sit up and concentrate. "I think we have much to discuss."

"I am willing to talk with the lord Grahame," returned Absu evenly, "if the lord Grahame will declare with hands on head and heart, swearing by the sacred robe, that there is nothing of deceit or treachery in his words."

Feeling somewhat foolish, Grahame placed one hand on his forehead and one on his chest. "Like this?"

Absu mes Marur nodded. "Such is the custom."

"I swear," said Grahame solemnly, "by the sacred robe that there is nothing of deceit or treachery in what I have to say. I swear also that neither I nor my companions have any enmity toward the lord Absu mes Marur or his people."

"The lord Grahame is generous in his oath."

"Russell is my first name, and I understand that Absu is your first name. Is it proper for us to use these names to each other?"

"Only if we have made the bond."

"How can we make this bond?"

Absu mes Marur smiled. "With a sword or a lance or a poniard at each other's throats. Between sept lords it should properly be swords."

"I have no sword, but I wish to make the bond." He glanced at the weapon that had not left Absu's bedside since he had placed it there. "May we not manage with one sword only?"

"It has been known," conceded the knight, "but chiefly on the field of battle."

"My friend," said Grahame without humor, "I think we may regard ourselves as being, in this place, on the field of battle."

"So be it," said the knight. "Let us then draw blood."

With a surprisingly agile movement for one who was injured and lying in bed, Absu mes Marur gripped his sword, leaned forward, and pressed the point lightly into Grahame's throat.

Grahame felt a thin trickle of blood running down his neck. He gazed along a meter of razor-sharp metal into the fierce eyes of a man who could end his life by a slight jerk of the wrist. He did not move.

Absu mes Marur growled. "Here is one whom I cannot kill. Here is one upon whom I may turn my back. Here is one in whose presence I may sleep. Here is one with whom my women may speak. If I forget these things, may a shameful death remind me. Thus, by the robe, it shall be."

He put down the sword and gestured to Grahame to take it.

Grahame held it gingerly. He did not trust himself with it. He was afraid to place it too near Absu's neck.

"Draw blood!" snapped the knight. Seeing that Grahame was reluctant, he pushed his throat onto the tip of the blade, and a thin stream of blood began to flow. "Now repeat the bond!"

Looking along the blade into the eyes of his companion, he spoke the words. Oddly, he found them very moving. They were, after all, a most powerful incantation. For they could stop men killing each other.

When he had finished, he placed the sword by Absu's side.

"This means that we no longer need to fight each other?" he asked.

"It means that we must never meet in combat."

"Good. To your custom, Absu, let us add one from my country." He held out a hand and showed Absu mes Marur how to clasp it and shake it. "I give you my hand in friendship. . . . Now, if you are not too tired, I will tell you about my own country and how I and my companions were brought to this place. When I have done so, you shall tell me about yourself."

In as simple a way as possible he tried to describe the technological civilization of the industrialized countries of Earth. But when he spoke of flying machines, of machines that could cover great distances rapidly on land or sea, and of machines for communicating at a distance, he saw that Absu's understanding and credulity were at breaking point. Hastily he concluded with a description of their arrival on Erewhon in the plastic coffins and of their attempts at exploration.

"You are, then, a race of magicians?" Absu regarded him mistrustfully.

"No, Absu, we are not magicians. I think the main difference between us is that my people have had longer to work metals than your people. And the clever men among us discovered how to make machines that would do much of the work of men and beasts. . . . Now let me hear your story. There will be time enough for us both to think about these things."

So it was that Grahame, his head aching because Absu naïvely assumed much background knowledge on his part, learned of the fateful red spice caravan traveling from the Kingdom of Ullos to the Upper and Lower Kingdoms of

Gren Li. Absu had been in command of the whole entourage, which consisted of some thirty warriors, nine or ten merchants, about fifteen women, and more than thirty pulpuls—a sort of mixture of deer and horse—carrying spice and other goods. Absu had no idea how or when the attack, as he chose to define it, had taken place. In this respect his memories and those of his companions were just as hazy as the recollections of the terrestrials. All that he knew for certain was that the caravan had been five days out of Ullos and was making its way across the high and extensive mountain range that separated Ullos from the Upper and Lower Kingdoms.

The manner of their arrival on Erewhon was much the same as that of the terrestrials except that instead of a hotel there was a stout wooden keep, and instead of a supermarket there was a herd of pulpuls. The curious thing was that Absu had received his injuries in the same way that Gunnar had met his death—quite possibly even in the same pit.

Fortunately, on his exploratory jaunt Absu had been riding a pulpul, which had taken the brunt of the fall and had impaled itself on the sharpened stakes. Ironically, most of Absu's wounds were caused by the pulpul in its death throes. He evidently became unconscious for a time, but in the end he managed to stand on the remains of the pulpul and haul himself out of the pit.

Being half out of his mind with pain and shock, he had tried to find his way back to the safety of the keep, only to wind up in a place that seemed, as he put it, to have been fashioned in the country of the dead. The white faces of the people he met—it appeared he had not noticed Selene—only served to confirm his first impression that he was among demons or ghosts.

"You are not among magicians or demons or ghosts,"

said Grahame, when he had finished his account. "You are among people like yourselves, Absu. It is true that our skins are paler—though some of our people are also dark—and that we are taller and live in different ways. But we also are men and women. Like you, we have been taken from our own world and placed—"

"From your own world?" interrupted Absu. "You mean, do you not, from your own country?"

"No, from our own world."

Absu mes Marur laughed. There was a look of relief upon his face. "So you magicians do not know everything," he observed jovially. "Know, friend Russell, that there is only one world. It is at the center of all things, and the sun is its lantern. . . . You have already spoken some nonsense of a world beyond the stars and on the far side of the sun. But such cannot exist; for Earth is as it always was—the play-board of the gods."

Grahame was confounded for a moment. "You speak of Earth?"

"I speak of Earth, this stage whereon our games are played, where we were born and where we must die. It is the only place, Russell, where men can live. It is the only place in all the strange abundance that the gods have created."

Grahame gazed at him in perplexity. "What shape do you think this Earth is?"

Again Absu laughed. "So much for the great machines and the great wisdom of you magicians. Truly, you must live near to the rim and so to outer darkness. . . . Even children know the shape of the Earth. It is flat and round like a platter, and very great are its dimensions. It is, doubtless, filled with many countries and many strange peoples with strange customs. But both your race and mine, Russell, belong to this Earth. We are its children."

"Then tell me," said Russell helplessly, "what would happen if a man were to journey to the very end of the world?"

"He would fall off," said Absu. "He would fall into darkness and be seen no more by his fellows. Such is the punishment of folly."

"Absu, my friend," said Russell with a sigh. "I fear that both of us have much to learn."

12

Keep Marur was no more than about fifteen kilometers to the northwest. When Absu had more or less recovered from his wounds—and by terrestrial standards his powers of recovery were amazing—Russell and Anna escorted him home. Russell had wanted to make the journey with Absu by himself. He was worried that there might be other surprises in store for the occupants of the Erewhon Hilton. The People of the River, for example, might turn up in force; and from reports they seemed pretty tough customers. So Russell was against reducing garrison strength more than was vital.

But Anna was firm. Someone, she claimed, would have to go with him, if only to keep him company on the homeward journey. Absu himself was quick to point out that his people would provide an escort for the return journey. But being unused to arguing with women and noting that Russell as lord of his sept did not do too well at the task, he accepted defeat with as much grace as was possible for a warrior lord in a male-orientated culture. That is to say, he ignored her henceforth and confined all his remarks to Russell.

During the last few days of his stay with the terrestrials, Absu mes Marur became more convinced than ever that he was in the company of magicians. He was introduced to the wonders of electric lighting, wrist watches, modern plumbing, cameras, binoculars, and the amazing fact that it was possible for a woman to walk before a man.

He remained considerably puzzled by Russell's insistence that the terrestrials came from a separate world which they, too, called Earth. He was also puzzled by their apparent ability to speak both the high and low Gren Li tongues fluently, though their lips made strange shapes. Most of all, he was puzzled by their unwarlike demeanor and attitudes. Eventually he came to the conclusion that such people probably fought with magic rather than with honest weapons and therefore congratulated himself that he had entered the bond with the lord of this curious sept. If the sept lords could not meet in combat, it followed logically that their people could not meet in combat, also. This was annoying in one respect and comforting in another. Peace was not a thing to be endured lightly, but at least it was preferable to joining battle with those who could make bright white light appear at will or take food from a hollow piece of metal.

During his absence Russell appointed John Howard to act as his deputy. If he did not return, Howard was to assume permanent responsibility for the group unless he was deposed by a majority vote in favor of someone else.

Early in the morning, before they left for Keep Marur, an interesting and comforting discovery was made by Simone Michel, who was on stores duty. She found that packs of cigarettes had reappeared in the supermarket. Evidently the punishment for curiosity—if, indeed, it was a punishment and not some oversight—was ended.

The journey itself was uneventful. It took most of the day, not only because Absu was still too weak to travel quickly but because he lost his way once or twice, adding a few extra kilometers. In the end he seemed to rely chiefly upon sniffing.

When he asked Absu what scent he was following, Russell learned that he was tracking back along paths recently taken by pulpuls either running wild or being ridden. It did not matter which. The wild pulpuls usually herded close to the keep, and ridden pulpuls would clearly be going either to or from the keep.

Russell himself sniffed whenever he saw Absu dilating his nostrils. But he could smell nothing—perhaps because he did not know what scent he was trying to pick up.

The pulpul, it appeared, was as important to the warrior peoples of the Upper and Lower Kingdoms of Gren Li as the buffalo was to the American Indian and the reindeer to the Laplanders. It provided personal transport and was also a beast of burden. Its body yielded meat, and its hide yielded clothing. Its guts were used to manufacture ropes and bow strings. Its horns could be worked into utensils, ornaments, spoons, needles, and knives. Its hooves were a reputed aphrodisiac, its tail was a charm against evil spirits and its nose, dried and cured, offered comfort to a woman in time of the warrior's absence.

Keep Marur stood on a slight rise that was perhaps two hundred meters above the surrounding terrain. It was not far from a small stream to which the women had already worn a well-trodden path in their daily quest for fresh water. The keep itself was no more than a wooden tower enclosed by a high stockade. The top of the keep, which was perhaps twenty-five meters above ground level, was serrated rather in the manner of a primitive fortress. It was manned by a couple of armed sentinels. They noticed the approach of Absu and his companions while they were still more than two kilometers away, and a small party was sent out to investigate.

The three warriors comprising the party from the keep rode their pulpuls through the tall grasses at a terrific rate, skilfully avoiding small trees and other obstacles in their path. Absu, aware of their approach, began to walk with a more springy step and a more imperious manner.

Until the keep had been sighted, he had been content to march between Anna and Russell. But now he took the lead, walking three or four paces ahead of his companions.

Anna was uneasy. "I think a spiritual change is coming over our alien friend," she said softly to Russell. "Perhaps it would have been better if we had left him to finish the journey by himself. What if these people decide it would be a good thing to have extra manpower?"

Russell held her hand and exuded more confidence than he was feeling. "Absu has a very potent sense of honor," he reminded her. "Besides, he and I are supposed to be blood brothers, or something like that. I don't think for a moment that he would be prepared to break his bond."

"You are too trustful, Russell—a typical Western weakness."

"And you are too cynical—a typical Eastern reaction . . ." He grinned. "That is why we are so good for each other."

The possibility of further conversation was limited by the arrival of the Gren Li warriors, who rode their pulpuls, gripping the horns somewhat comically, almost as if they were bicycle handlebars, directly toward Absu mes Marur until it seemed that their intention was to trample him down.

However, the pulpuls' ability to stop suddenly was far better than that of horse or deer. At signals from their riders the three animals came to a halt simultaneously.

"From the children of Absu mes Marur, greetings," said one of the riders.

"From Absu mes Marur to his children, greetings also," returned Absu equably.

"Lord, it was feared that you had perished."

"I have been near enough to death to taste the flavor, but I was restored by my enemy's enemy."

"Lord"—a lance swung casually in the direction of Russell's stomach—"these strangers are the fruit of conquest?"

"They are the fruit of friendship. It is at their hands that I live. If any call this weakness, let him now make the challenge according to his ancient rights."

The three men muttered softly to each other, then the one who was clearly their spokesman turned to Absu mes Marur. "We do not question the valor or the wisdom of our sept lord. By the robe, this is so."

"Nor is your own wisdom doubted," replied Absu. "Now dismount, my children, for these my guests shall ride."

Despite Russell's protestations, he and Anna were helped on to the pulpuls and were shown how to grip the horns. The beasts were surprisingly easy to ride, perhaps because they kept their heads erect and so gave steady support to the rider.

The rest of the journey to the keep took no more than a few minutes, the pulpuls jogging sedately along and the "children" of Absu mes Marur running by their sides. As they went up the rise on which the keep stood, a few notes —not unpleasing to terrestrial ears—sounded out a welcome from some kind of trumpet or horn.

Keep Marur, constructed like the Erewhon Hilton and the supermarket by unknown hands, had been in existence before the arrival of its occupants—which, Russell discovered, was about the time that the terrestrials themselves had arrived. As with the hotel and the supermarket, great care had been taken to ensure that the keep was typical of the kind of building to which its occupants had been accustomed.

Externally it was a gloomy edifice, with a number of small triangular windows for each of the different floor levels. Inside, at least above the first level, it was surprisingly comfortable, with neatly stitched pulpul skins covering the wooden floors and with piles of furs and even a few fabric-covered cushions for sitting or lying on. Weapons and trophies hung on the walls, and smoky lamps—burning pulpul oil—lent a flickering homeliness to the otherwise dark apartments.

The first level of the keep seemed to be a combined butchery, bakery, armory, and general workshop. From this area wooden steps led up to the door of the women's apartments, then to the merchants' and warriors' quarters, and finally to the sept lord's own apartment directly below the battlement.

It was here, after Absu had ceremonially shown his guests to the remainder of his "children"—guest-showing being a ritual of practical value in a society where the appearance of strangers was itself sufficient to provoke violence—that Anna and Russell were entertained.

During his stay with the terrestrials Absu had been forced to come to terms with canned milk and strange preserved foods. Now it was the turn of the terrestrials to accustom their stomachs to strange foods. They were served with what looked and tasted rather like chopped avocado pear but which, in fact, turned out to be raw pulpul brains—one of the greatest delicacies that could be offered. This was followed by braised pulpul heart, some not unpleasant vegetables, and the red spice of which Russell had already heard.

He had imagined, from Absu's description, that red spice would be something similar to pepper. He was right—and wrong. It was much hotter than any pepper he had ever known, causing beads of sweat to form on his forehead.

Also, it was terribly intoxicating, but not until one drank water.

Surprisingly, Anna was able to take the red spice fairly well. It was, as they discovered by watching Absu, eaten in tiny spoonfuls (pulpul-horn spoons) from a central dish, alternately with mouthfuls of tough, bitter pulpul heart. Russell drank freely from the water that was offered him by a small, brown, almost naked woman who squatted next to him and laid her hands on his shoulders in a somewhat familiar fashion. Apart from the woman, who was strikingly beautiful even by terrestrial standards, and who was called Yasal, no one from Absu's sept was present.

By the end of the meal Russell was drunk. He knew he was drunk and felt very foolish.

Absu mes Marur regarded him solemnly. "I had hoped this evening that we should speak again of many things which trouble us both, Russell." He glanced at the bowl of red spice. "But I fear the journey has fatigued each of us in different ways. Let us then preserve our serious thoughts until we rise refreshed with the sun. Meanwhile, as is our custom, my woman shall warm your skins, and your woman shall warm mine."

Through the fog of drunkenness Russell dimly perceived that the hospitality of this medieval sept lord carried with it some rather startling implications. He looked at Anna, who was gazing at Absu mes Marur stony-faced.

Then he turned to his host. "Abshu, ol' sport. We have a problem." He paused, groping for the right words. "In my country, we do not exchange women. . . . Well, not much."

Absu smiled. "Nor do we, Russell, my friend—except during the first night of the first visit only. It is the custom of the keeps and a bond token. So it has always been. So, doubtless, it will always be. . . . As for myself, I have little enthusiasm for one who is tall and ghostly and knows not how to respect her lord. But the custom of the keeps is sacred, and I fear you have the best of it."

Anna Markova, however, was not to be discountenanced by a retrogressive, uncouth, alien, medieval autocrat. To give herself time to think of an adequately crushing retort, she took a deep draft of water after her final spoonful of red spice.

It was her undoing. The mysterious vapors of the red spice, in immediate reaction, seemed to rise from her stomach directly to her brain, there becoming incandescent and cauterizing all rational thought.

"Know this, Absu mes Marur," she said thickly. "A free Russian woman is worth any ten of the unemancipated sluts who pass for females in your little entourage. Personally, I have no inclination to lie with bloodthirsty pygmies, but in the interests of international—correction—interplanetary relations, I will warm your skins in such a fashion that you will remember it with wonder for the rest of your days."

Russell was appalled, Yasal's eyes widened with amazement, and Absu laughed so much he almost did himself an injury.

"By the robe, by the white queen and the black, this ghost woman has a remarkable spirit," he said to Russell. "But know, my friend, that she does herself too much honor. The heat of her blood is surely no match for the heat of her words."

Anna stood up—with difficulty—and gazed down scornfully at the Gren Li sept lord. "Barbarian," she said, groping for the right insults. "Savage. Imperialist. Fascist. I will teach you to respect your intellectual and moral superiors if it is the last thing—"

Her eyes clouded. She tried to keep them open, but the

eyelids appeared to be obeying some higher authority. She swayed soundlessly, then collapsed in a heap.

Absu mes Marur grinned. "It is as I said. You, Russell, will have the best of it." He grabbed Anna by an arm and a handful of hair and dragged her with some difficulty to a pile of skins. "Certainly like this she will be less of a nuisance."

But as he turned back to the food mat, Russell himself slumped in a heap.

Absu mes Marur gave Yasal, his chief night woman, a despairing glance. "These, though friends, are not familiar with our ways. You know your duty, child. Go to it."

13

Late on the following afternoon Russell and Anna, their heads still aching a little, were escorted back toward home —strange how they had suddenly begun to think of the Erewhon Hilton as home—by two of Absu's warriors. All four of them rode pulpuls, and the journey was accomplished quickly and without incident.

As they jogged along, holding tightly onto the ridiculous horn handlebars and flanked by the Gren Li warriors, Russell's mind turned to the conversation that had passed between him and Absu mes Marur during the morning— after he and Anna had disposed of their post-binge shakes with long drafts of water and a few flakes of what passed for unleavened bread.

Among the people who had been abducted from the red spice caravan there was a man whom Absu had referred to as the pathfinder. In the Upper and Lower Kingdoms, where trade depended upon the efficient routing of caravans over difficult, changing, and sometimes featureless terrain, the art of pathfinding was an ancient and honored profession, jealously confined to a few families.

Absu's pathfinder was also something of a mapmaker and an explorer. Shortly after their arrival at Keep Marur, he had been dispatched to explore the country to the north, which, being hilly, might be more attractive than the lowlands. Absu mes Marur and his people normally preferred hill country; and if the high land did not have any serious drawbacks, he was prepared to abandon Keep Marur and build a new one in a place more to his liking.

The pathfinder went alone on his expedition and was away nearly three days. He returned with some curious information. Wild animals abounded to the north, therefore the land was good for hunting. Though, he added, some of the beasts he had seen might prey upon the pulpuls. This was a serious limitation, since any threat to the pulpuls constituted a threat to the group's entire way of life.

The pathfinder also maintained that he had seen savages and what he described as a swarm of winged demons whose faces seemed to be covered by long golden hair. He had not had any opportunity to study them closely or for more than a few moments, since, though the demons were flying low, they traveled very quickly and were soon lost to sight.

The pathfinder must have been a very courageous man, because this experience did not deter him from making his way across the range of hills that he had reached. On the other side he discovered a fairly even plain where, in contrast to the side he had left, the grass and vegetation were poor and sparse. Enclosing the plain and transforming it into the segment of a vast circle there was a high and apparently static wall of mist or fog.

Mindful of his professional pride and his duty to his sept lord, the pathfinder resisted the temptation to turn back there and then. He marched across the plain on foot, leaving his pulpul tethered to a shrub. He had to do this for the simple reason that the pulpul, normally docile and obedient, refused to go forward.

It did not take the pathfinder long to reach the wall of mist. As he approached, he confidently expected that the strange barrier would no longer look like a wall. He was wrong. Though there was some breeze, the mist barrier remained motionless and definite in shape.

The curiosity of the pathfinder proved to be a stronger stimulus than his fear of this abnormal phenomenon. He hoped to pass through the white wall of mist if he could and to discover what lay on the other side. But before he entered it, he stood for some time gazing at the mist, noting several strange facts.

Its "surface" was not fluffy or irregular as one might expect from a wave of ordinary ground or sea mist. It was uniform and opaque. It did not merge or mingle with the atmosphere at all and seemed almost as if it were held in position by an invisible and rigid skin. The wall stretched away into the distance on each side of the pathfinder, and looking along it, he could see that the curvature was uniform.

Being an enterprising and intelligent fellow, the pathfinder did some rough but intricate calculations based upon the assumptions that the curvature remained constant and that the wall itself did not end. If that were the case, he reasoned, he and his sept and the land to which they had been brought would be contained in a circle of perhaps fifty or sixty varaks in diameter. (In discussion with Absu, Russell had been able to establish that one kilometer was roughly equal to one and a half varaks.)

Dwelling upon the implications of this possibility, the pathfinder came to the conclusion that it was his plain duty to penetrate the mist. Though brave, he was a naturally cautious man—as befitting his art—and instead of plunging boldly into the mist, he first of all put his hand into it.

The hand disappeared almost as if it had been cut off at the wrist. Holding his hand in the mist for a few moments, the pathfinder became aware of a faint tingling in his

fingers. When at last he withdrew the hand, it was noticeably cooler than the rest of his body.

The pathfinder meditated on these discoveries for a
while. They did nothing to improve his confidence. If the
mist were so opaque as to make his hand disappear, how
could he possibly find his bearings once he himself entered
it?

However, besides having a lodestone, which was part of
his standard equipment, he also carried with him a length
of twine almost one-quarter of a varak long, made out of
twisted pulpul hair. In case the lodestone should fail him
—and who could foresee what effect such a mist would
have on a simple lodestone?—he planted his lance securely
in the ground and tied one end of the twine around it and
the other end around his waist.

The precautions were unnecessary. He was unable to
penetrate far into the mist wall, and it was quite easy for
him to find his way back. He was unable to penetrate
deeply because with every step he took it became noticeably and uncomfortably colder. After half a dozen steps
frost formed on his skin; after three more steps he could
not move his fingers; after two more steps his lips froze
together, and a film of ice was beginning to form over his
eyes. Finding his way out was simple. He had only to seek
comparative warmth.

Mindful of his duty to his sept lord, the pathfinder tried
to pass through a different part of the mist wall. Again he
was driven back by the intense cold. He tried a third time
and was driven back once more. Then, sensibly, he gave
up, made his way back to where he had left the pulpul,
and returned to Keep Marur to relate his experiences and
make a rough map of his journey.

Russell heard the story from Absu when he had recovered from his red spice hangover. He asked if he could

question the pathfinder himself. But before Absu's return to the keep the man had been dispatched to look for his sept lord and had not yet returned.

As the two terrestrials and the Gren Li warriors journeyed back to the Erewhon Hilton, Russell considered the significance of the pathfinder's story.

Granted the zoo hypothesis, and granting the supposition that the mist wall continued to form an unbroken circle, one was left with the conclusion that however large the reservation area was—and it might even be as much as nine hundred square kilometers—the zoo keepers had no intention of letting their "animals" escape. On the other hand, the pathfinder could easily be wrong in his conclusions; and the freezing mist might well be a local phenomenon.

But remembering the report John Howard had brought back from the second expedition, Russell was inclined to believe that Absu's pathfinder had interpreted the purpose of the mist barrier correctly. While Howard was studying the People of the River through his binoculars, he had discerned a high, unmoving wall of fog in the distance, on the far side of the river. It seemed highly probable that this mist barrier and the pathfinder's barrier were one and the same. Since the pathfinder had gone in a northerly direction and John Howard's party had explored in a southerly direction, the notion of a circular wall was considerably strengthened.

In which case, several interesting possibilities were revealed. . . .

Suddenly Russell was aware that Anna was talking to him.

"We are very near home now, Russell. I do not think our warrior friends need accompany us all the way to our base" —she glanced significantly at the two impassive riders—

"so perhaps we could walk the last kilometer or two on foot."

"You are quite right," said Russell, taking the hint. Although Absu mes Marur was familiar enough with the Erewhon Hilton, there was little point in letting his warlike followers see for themselves how indefensible it was from a military viewpoint. It might give them ideas.

He halted his pulpul and spoke to the two warriors. "My friends, it has pleased the lord Absu to send you to accompany us to our own land. For this we are grateful. We wish now to continue the last part of our journey on foot. Therefore, with thanks, we return to you the pulpuls we have ridden. Say to your lord that we have greatly enjoyed his company and that we thank him and you for the protection he has given on our homeward journey."

Russell dismounted carefully—realizing that it would bring great loss of face if he were to fall off a pulpul—and helped Anna to dismount from her beast.

"Lord Russell," said one of the warriors, "we hear you and obey. But know that our sept lord commanded us to see you safely to your keep, and it will go ill with us if harm should come to you because we have not discharged this task."

"No harm will come to us," said Russell. "But say to the lord Absu that I commanded you to return at this point."

The warriors saluted, slapping their hands upon the blades of their weapons. "By the sacred robe it shall be. Farewell."

"In the name of the white queen and the black," replied Russell gravely, exercising his small knowledge of the strange idiom, "go safely."

The warriors swung their pulpuls around, the two riderless creatures following them obediently, and cantered off back along the route they had recently taken.

Russell and Anna began to walk forward hand in hand. It was a hot afternoon, and there was plenty of time before sunset, so they were not inclined to hurry.

After a time, the greenness of the savanna and the stillness of the air filled them with lassitude. They found a knoll on which the grass was comparatively short and sat down to rest. They lay there for a while, gazing at the blue sky and a few fleecy and thoroughly normal-looking clouds.

Anna was the first to speak. "Russell. Last night . . . Did you—did you fraternize with that attractive little savage?"

He gazed at her in bewilderment. "Do you know, I really can't remember. How odd!"

Anna smiled. "I think she would not have been easy to forget."

"I still can't remember. . . . That red spice and water combination makes a-hundred-and-forty-proof Polish white spirit seem like lemonade. . . . And you, Anna. Did you —er—fraternize with Absu?"

She looked at him calmly. "I, too, don't know. . . . But there were signs that . . . Well, I think I may have done. . . . That red spice was certainly powerful."

Russell burst out laughing. "All I remember is that you called him a lot of terrible names and then fell flat on your face."

Anna reddened. "I am trying to be serious," she said stiffly. "If either of us did, there may be certain genetic possibilities."

Again Russell laughed. "Don't, you are putting me on heat. . . . I'm sorry, my dear. I'll try to be serious."

"It is not a subject for laughing at," she pointed out.

"I know. . . . But it's a hot day, we've had a crazy adventure, we are near home, and you look delicious." He placed his hand on her breast.

Her nose wrinkled. "Shall we fraternize?" she asked solemnly.

"Sweetheart, let us do that thing."

Then, without any further need for conversation, and amid the great green silence of the savanna, they made love. Presently they picked themselves up and strolled lazily back to the Erewhon Hilton. It had been a day to remember.

14

That evening Russell called a general meeting in the hotel dining room. He told his companions all that had happened, omitting only the pleasant little interlude with Anna shortly before journey's end.

Everyone was amused and intrigued by their experiences; and before any serious discussion began there was a barrage of ribald comments and questions. When it eventually died down, John Howard raised the conversation to a more constructive level.

"I take it you think we ought to consider our situation in the light of recent events," he said.

Russell nodded. "We still know very little, and not enough to make much sense; but I think we ought to put our heads together and see if we can't come up with a few reasonable deductions. After all, it begins to look as if we may be here one hell of a long time; and our survival—or otherwise—may depend on how we react to the information we have acquired so far."

Marion Redman said, "You think these people really are human beings, Russell?"

Russell shrugged. "How does one define human beings, Marion? Are they creatures who live only on Earth—I should say *our* Earth? If so, then Absu mes Marur and company are not human beings. But their appearance and *my* instinct tell me that they are definitely human. Nonterrestrial human, certainly. But still human. Which, of course, evades the question."

"Perhaps Anna will be able to enlighten us in nine months," suggested Mohan das Gupta solemnly.

"Point taken." Russell winked at Anna. "But what if the baby looks like a British left-wing politician?"

Simone Michel suddenly threw in a novel thought. "Suppose they don't exist?" she said. "Suppose we are having a mass hallucination or something like that?"

"Suppose, also, that we are all still on the plane from Stockholm to London," observed John Howard drily. "We are all taking part in a cosy communal dream, but presently we shall be passing through the Customs at Heathrow. . . . No, once we start this line of thought, we can admit all kinds of extravagant notions."

"It *is* possible," persisted Simone, tossing her long dark hair. "I know it is crazy. But then everything that has happened to us is crazy. Therefore it is possible."

"Simone has a thought," said Paul Redman.

"Driven home with some wonderfully refutable Gallic logic," added John. "No. I think that with so many imponderables we must apply the principle that the simplest explanation is most probably the correct one. So . . . We were physically removed from the jet, the surroundings in which we find ourselves are real, the things that have happened to us are real—and let us not forget that Gunnar and Marina are dead—and the people we have met are real. From that base we can begin to draw conclusions."

"Let's not forget the People of the River," said Robert Hyman.

"Or the metal spiders," added Selene Bergere, shivering.

"Or Paul's fairies," said Tore Norstedt. "Who, please, has taken my bottle of whiskey?"

"Order, ladies and gents all," said Russell. "This discussion is in danger of disappearing in a singular fashion. . . . John, you have the look of somebody who has something to say. So how about giving us your interpretation of events?"

John smiled. "It won't take as long as you think, because really I am just as baffled as everyone else. But we do have some facts and a few interesting theories, so perhaps the time for speculation is ripe. Until something better comes along, the zoo theory is the best we have. So let's accept it for the time being. Now, who runs the zoo? We don't know. We know that robots are involved because we have evidence. I cannot believe that these robots are anything more than comparatively simple servants of the people or creatures who put us here. Maybe these spider robots are controlled by more complex machines, and it's even possible that the whole exercise is computer-controlled with a degree of sophistication that we can't begin to imagine. But again, I prefer the simpler explanation that the project is the work of a biological species and not, as it were, an electromechanical species."

"I think my fairies are our overlords," said Paul Redman seriously.

His suggestion was greeted by a burst of laughter. Nervous laughter.

"I'll come to that in a minute," said John. "And I, personally, don't think the idea is as crazy as most of you do. But bear with me for a few more minutes. . . . We know that we are being watched, but we have no contact with the watchers. This could mean that they are naturally secretive, that direct contact with us might invalidate their experiment or operation, that they are afraid of being seen, or that they think we may be afraid of them. You pays your penny and you takes your choice. I incline to the view that they think contact would affect the operation. The only thing we can be certain of is that they are interested in our welfare, because they have taken a great deal of trouble to provide us with a comfortable environment and the kind of food to which we are accustomed."

"There is also the possibility," put in Robert Hyman drily, "that the entire project may be a variation on the theme of fattening the geese for Christmas."

"Cannibalism?" exploded Selene, her wide eyes rolling.

"Not, perhaps, in the literal sense," said John obscurely. "Yes, Robert, there is certainly the possibility that we may be experimental rabbits—but not, I think, in the sense of being used for vivisection or tested to destruction. . . . What do we really know, so far? We know that there are at least two alien social groups—alien to this planet, that is —ours and the Gren Li people. And where the Gren Li contingent came from we have not the faintest clue, because they still think they are on their own world—I suppose it is still remotely possible for that to be the case—which they believe to be flat and at the center of the cosmos. We know that they, like us, have been subjected to some quite astounding operation that enables us all to communicate with each other, regardless of language. We also know—or think we know—that they are human. . . . And, though we have not yet established direct contact with the People of the River, I am convinced that they too have shared this common experience of abduction and that they too will be apparently able to speak English, Swedish, or the Gren Li language as the occasion demands."

"They also seem to be pretty handy with deep pits and sharp stakes," observed Andrew Payne grimly.

"Certainly. Hunting is probably their most important pursuit. It seems fairly certain that the pits are meant primarily for animals and not humans. . . . Now, granted this hypothesis about the People of the River, we have three radically different social groups from entirely different worlds, able to communicate with each other and enclosed in the same area. I believe, as Absu mes Marur's bright pathfinder suspected, that the mist wall extends most likely for a complete circle and represents, in fact, the bars of our very large cage. . . . Within this cage we have samples of a Stone Age culture, a medieval culture, and a technological culture. Perhaps somebody just wants to see what happens. . . . Which brings me back to Paul's fairies or, if you like, the pathfinder's winged demons."

"John," said Mohan das Gupta, "you are a good chap, but you have fallen off your trolley. Why invoke these bloody fairies or demons or whatever?"

"Because," said John Howard impressively, "they are the only creatures so far encountered that can obviously pass over the wall."

15

For a few minutes the discussion degenerated into a free-for-all concerning the existence, nature, purpose, or potential of the alleged fairies or demons. Russell saw that it wasn't going to get anywhere, for the simple reason that there was no objective evidence that could be fruitfully discussed. Paul had only caught a glimpse of the creatures, and so had the Gren Li pathfinder. Indeed, it was possible if not probable that each had seen different types of winged creatures. And until such beings could either be inspected at close range or for long periods, or preferably both, all was wild surmise. The winged beings existed, and presumably they could fly over the wall. But that, contrary to John Howard's conviction, proved nothing. If the fairies or demons were intelligent observers, they were being very discreet about it.

So Russell nursed his gin and tonic and waited for the humor and wild fantasy to die down. At length, he judged the time was ripe for his own contribution.

"May I toss in a few words?" he began. "John has led us—with some pretty sound observations *en route*—into the deep blue yonder. I would like to bring us back to Earth, or at least back to our little zoo on Erewhon. Let us assume that the People of the River are in the same predicament as ourselves and the occupants of Keep Marur. We have, then, as John suggested, three types of culture in the same cage—and all human, for want of a better word. Whoever set it up is clearly interested in our interaction—

and so am I. One thing I am sure of is that we cannot remain isolationist. We must pool our resources and experience, even with the Stone Age boys, if we can."

"I imagine those people play rough," said Paul Redman gloomily. "If they are true Stone Age types, they are probably loaded with taboo, bloodlust, and xenophobia. The first character who tries to shake hands will be asking for a headful of flint ax."

"Possibly," conceded Russell. "In which case we must find out as much about them as we can before we try making any overtures. More observation from a distance, and all that sort of thing. If necessary, we could enlist the aid of our medieval friends. . . . But there is also another project—perhaps more valuable—to which we should give some thought."

"What is that?" asked Mary Howard.

"Escape," answered Russell.

"From Erewhon?"

"From the zoo. We have plenty of space and very little to complain of. But I don't like the idea of being confined, and I do want to know what is on the other side of this supposedly impenetrable barrier."

"If we are to believe the medievals, their pathfinder had a pretty harrowing experience," said Robert Hyman. "Personally, I wouldn't care to have my eyeballs frozen."

"I have been thinking about that," said Russell, "and I think that there may be a way we can get out, and in, without too much damage. . . . We know that a river runs through our little reservation and—"

"Of course!" said John Howard.

Russell laughed. "Please, John, let me deliver my own punch lines. It is a pretty big river, and I am willing to bet that it does not rise in the relatively small range of hills that we know about. We will have to check by exploration, but I think that the river will cut the mist barrier at two points. There will be a point of entry and a point of exit. So if we build a boat or raft, we ought to be able to just drift out of the zoo."

"What about the rapid temperature loss?" asked Tore Norstedt.

"A problem," admitted Russell, "but not, I think, insoluble. Absu's pathfinder was totally unprepared for his experience. We know what to expect, so we could provide ourselves with lots of insulation. If necessary, I think we could completely enclose the boat and bury ourselves under piles of clothing. If my theory about the river is okay and if the mist barrier is not very wide, we should be able to pass through it before the cold really hits."

"There is a pretty good way of assessing the risk," said John Howard excitedly.

"What's that?"

"We have to find where the river comes through the mist barrier. Then we test the water temperature and compare it with temperatures downstream. If we measure the rate of flow and check the temperatures at different depths, we ought to be able to make an enlightened guess about how thick the mist barrier is, or at least how long it would take for a drifting boat to get through it."

"Thank the Lord for science teachers," said Russell reverently. "If the project is feasible, we have a lot of work on our hands. We have to establish contact and make our peace with the People of the River, if only because the boat will have to pass through their territory. We have to find where the river comes in and where it goes out. And then we have to design and build a boat and equip our intrepid explorers, if any."

"The hell with all that," said Mohan languidly. "Why don't we just take it easy and wait for something to happen?

Sooner or later something is bound to happen. The chaps who brought us here are going to get tired of just supplying our groceries. Sooner or later they will want a return on investment."

"That is the thought that troubles me," retorted Russell. "As a decadent western pseudo-intellectual," he grinned at Anna, "I am all for comfort and security. But at the same time, I would like—if possible—to find out what the whole thing is about before somebody decides it's time to switch the program."

"What if there's nothing beyond the mist barrier but more bloody grassland and forest and hills stretching into the far distance?"

"Even that information would be useful."

"What if one or more of us gets hurt or killed trying to break out?"

Russell shrugged. "That is a risk we have to take. I wouldn't want such an expedition to consist of more than two people—me being one."

Mohan smiled and poured himself another drink. "Your trouble, Russell, is that you are a bloody hero. The archetypal Englishman—thin red line vintage."

"My trouble," said Russell, "is that, like the Elephant's Child, I have an insatiable curiosity."

16

During the next few weeks several interesting—and some frightening—things happened. Ever since he had suggested the aim of ultimately passing through the mist barrier to explore the world outside, Russell noticed that the morale of his thirteen companions had improved perceptibly. Up till that time they had felt helpless in a situation that they could neither understand nor do anything about. But now they had a purpose—a real, if limited, objective. It was enough to dispel the insidious mental lassitude that had imperceptibly sapped their energies and their willpower.

One of the small but ultimately important things that happened was that one of the British students, Janice Blake, managed to rear some chickens. She had been brought up on a small East Anglian poultry farm, and she was very homesick. It occurred to her one day that some of the eggs that were nocturnally delivered to the supermarket by the indefatigable metal spiders might possibly be fertile. So she made a straw box and rigged a low-power electric light bulb wrapped in some discarded clothing to provide the heat normally supplied by a broody hen. She kept the box of straw and the simple heating appliance in one of the spare rooms of the Erewhon Hilton. Each morning she added two eggs to the clutch, each pair of eggs taken from a different batch at the supermarket. On the twenty-third day of her experiment, she was rewarded by a chicken hatching. Another came out on the thirty-fourth day and two more on the fortieth day. One of the chickens later revealed itself as a cock, and in the end Janice's experiment yielded some very useful and rewarding results.

Meanwhile, Robert Hyman had appointed himself official weapon maker. He had already equipped the men with longbows; but archery was clearly not a common talent. Apart from Robert himself, no one could use the longbow with any degree of accuracy. So he designed a simple crossbow, or arbalest, that used a short but heavy bolt. He made the crossbow so that it could be used also with some effect by the women, and when he had found the best balance between power and ease of use, he put the crossbow into mass production. He spent most of his days in one of the small workshops beside the hotel, turning out a dozen crossbows and a large number of bolts. In the evenings, just before dinner, the group would indulge in target practice under his instruction. After a time even the women were able to hit a target the size of a man at thirty paces.

When he had satisfied himself that the crossbows and bolts could be used effectively by everybody, Robert began work on a more ambitious project. He began to design a large but portable ballista. He had talked the matter over with Russell. Crossbows, hatchets, and knives were fine as weapons for personal combat or protection; but an occasion might arise—if, for example, there was some serious difference of opinion with the occupants of Keep Marur—where a long-range engine of destruction was required. The ballista that Robert was proposing to build could be handled and transported by three men and should be able to hurl a ten-pound missile about half a kilometer. In short, it could be used against a large target that was well out of bowshot range.

Recalling his visit to Keep Marur, Russell was confident that the Gren Li people only had light personal weapons.

Regarding the ballista as a form of insurance, he was therefore much in favor of a weapon that could give some
strategic advantage. Although he hoped that the friendship
and the bond that existed between himself and Absu mes
Marur would prevent any serious clash, he was not so naïve
as to rely on it entirely. Besides, something might happen
to Absu; and his successor might not feel bound to honor
the friendship. The Gren Li people were environmentally
conditioned to be fierce and warlike. If it came to a clash
involving close-range weapons, they would very soon make
short work of the terrestrials.

So the ballista began to take shape.

While this project was under way, John Howard made an
important discovery. He found, quite by accident, a large
patch of ground that was naturally rich in saltpeter. By the
slow and arduous process of getting it out of the soil and
into a solution and then crystallizing it out of the solution,
he managed, during the course of several days of digging
and separating, to produce about five kilograms of fairly
pure saltpeter. Access to sulphur was easy. It was in the
supermarket for medicinal purposes. All he now needed
was charcoal, and that could be obtained by heating wood
in an enclosed container.

His first gunpowder mixture was too coarse and only
fizzled. But when Mary had ground the charcoal and the
sulphur to a very fine powder—oddly, this was the hardest
part of the entire business—John produced a gunpowder
that was very potent indeed. With such gunpowder it
would be possible to make simple grenades. And grenades,
like the ballista, were another piece of insurance.

Warlike activities did not, however, predominate. Cautious and systematic exploration was undertaken, particularly toward the south and the territory of the People of
the River. Russell did not think that the time was yet ripe

for a confrontation with such primitive people. He thought it probable that they would fight first and ask questions afterward, as it were. So he wanted to be sure that the terrestrials could deal with any aggression before he risked holding out the hand of friendship.

But this did not preclude observation. And although the People of the River would undoubtedly be stronger on forest lore—therefore dangerous in wooded country—if the terrestrial observers kept as much as possible to open ground and made good use of their binoculars, the risk of a surprise encounter should not be too high. Paul and Marion Redman, Andrew Payne, and Selene Bergere trained together and formed themselves into a semipermanent exploration force. Both Paul and Andrew became reasonably good shots with the crossbow; and Selene, who was not very good with mechanical or even semimechanical things, devised her own weapon. It was a derivation of the South American bola—two large stones joined together by a meter of cord. Selene learned to swing and fling with surprising accuracy, so that she could bring a running man down at distances of up to forty meters.

So, with crossbows, bolas, and hatchets for protection against man or beast, the exploration force made three successful trips to study the People of the River. As on the first occasion when the People of the River were seen, they maintained a respectable distance and did most of their spying with the binoculars. They counted—or thought they counted—a total of ten adults and four largish children.

The People of the River were shaggy in every way, and it was virtually impossible to distinguish males from females. During the daytime they seemed to stay pretty close to their bridge of huts, busying themselves with simple tasks, relaxing and sleeping, and even occasionally indulging in what looked like simple games. They were obviously hunters—and most probably nocturnal hunters. No doubt they also ate any wild fruit or plants that were palatable; but fresh meat was clearly their main diet.

On their second expedition the terrestrials saw for themselves the kind of animal that was trapped by the People of the River. While they were observing the bridge of huts from a vantage point fairly near to the river itself, they heard a great commotion in a large patch of trees that straggled out from the main part of the forest behind them. Paul and Andrew decided to investigate. They found a creature that looked rather like a particularly vicious wild boar. It had evidently just sprung a trap and was now suspended untidily in a large, tough net that hung between two young trees. The boar—if such it was—had a mate, who was growling and leaping up and down helplessly. When the mate saw the two terrestrials, it charged instantly and was only brought down by a very lucky shot from Paul's crossbow. The bolt had completely disappeared inside the animal's chest, but it still refused to die, and the two men had to finish it off with hatchets.

That the People of the River were not entirely nocturnal in their aggressive habits was discovered in a frightening fashion by Selene Bergere on the third expedition. She had wandered away from the other three to attend to the needs of nature and had found a small hollow where both tasks could be performed in relative comfort. The forest was unusually quiet, and it was this that probably saved Selene's life, together with the fact that several of the nearby trees had shed many of their leaves.

The Stone Age man came running up behind her with far greater speed than any terrestrial could have done. But Selene heard the crackle of the dry fallen leaves and had just enough time to turn and fling her bola. The cord wrapped itself around his legs and brought him down with a grunt. Selene fled screaming. When the others reached her—and it did not take more than a few seconds—they all went back to investigate. There was no sign of the savage or of the bola.

While these exciting activities were going on, Tore Norstedt occupied himself by building a tough, flat-bottomed boat of very shallow draft. It was designed to carry a maximum of four people, and it was to be propelled by short wooden paddles. Oars would have been more efficient, perhaps, for long, clear stretches of water. But the course and characteristics of the river had not yet been explored properly. Almost certainly there would be shallows and rapids where paddles could be put to good use.

Bearing in mind that the boat would have to carry its occupants through the mist barrier, whose depth and maximum coldness had yet to be calculated, Tore equipped his boat with a small, detachable cabin, the walls of which were to be insulated by blankets and straw.

It was while Tore was working on his boat one day that he hit upon an idea which, surprisingly, had not occurred to anyone else. Or perhaps it had occurred to some of the others and been rejected because of the element of risk involved.

The supermarket, as had already been discovered, was frequently restocked by robots. No one had seen these machines, despite a nocturnal guard being maintained, until Andrew Payne unexpectedly came across one in the small hours. Subsequently, Andrew's "great spiders" had been photographed—and the terrestrials had been penalized for their curiosity by having their cigarette supply temporarily curtailed. But, apart from an annoying absence of cigarettes, no drastic action had been taken.

Since that time the night guard had been maintained. But the metal spiders had not been seen again. To Tore

Norstedt, this seemed to reinforce his original theory that the zoo keepers could "switch off" the terrestrials in some manner whenever they wished.

It occurred to Tore that the robots probably had to bring their supplies in through the mist barrier somehow—unless there was a subterranean stockpile—and that if it were possible to follow one of them on the return journey, an easy way out of the zoo might be found.

He proposed to arrange a trip string and buzzer, as had been used for the taking of the photograph. Only this time, instead of the buzzer being in Tore's room in the hotel and linked to his traveling clock, both he and the buzzer would be concealed in the supermarket. The buzzer would serve simply to wake him up if he should fall asleep.

Also attached to the trip string would be a lasso with small, multiple nooses, the other end of the lasso being secured around Tore's waist. The spiders had four feet and four arms. Tore was sure he could arrange the nooses in such a way that it would be virtually impossible for a robot to enter the supermarket without entangling one or more of its appendages. Once that happened, wherever the spider went —even if the night were dark and the terrain difficult—Tore would be able to follow.

That, at least, was the theory. Tore said nothing about his plan to Russell or, indeed, to anyone. He had a naïve and childish desire to be able to stroll in at breakfast time and say casually, "Oh, by the way, I have found out where the robots come from, and I think there is an easy way through the mist barrier."

So he made his multiple lasso very carefully out of tough wire and, late on the night that he chose for his experiment, invented some story about a special guard duty for the benefit of Andrea and Janice, with whom he had developed a more or less permanent and surprisingly successful *ménage à trois*.

Then he took himself across to the supermarket, set the trap, and hid himself discreetly behind a stack of cereal packages.

As he left the hotel, he briefly exchanged a word with Anna Markova, whom he met returning after a short evening walk.

And that was the last that anyone saw of him alive.

17

Absu mes Marur and his pathfinder, a small wiry man, darker and yet even more Mongolian in features than his master, brought back to the Erewhon Hilton what was left of Tore Norstedt. They rode their pulpuls up to the hotel late one afternoon when a pleasantly cool breeze was blowing away the little drifts of feathery seeds that had been accumulating, despite frequent attempts at clearance, for several weeks.

The battered, barely recognizable, and half-severed body of Tore Norstedt was slung across the back of the pathfinder's pulpul. Janice was the first to see it and mercifully fainted after uttering a thin and heartrending scream.

As the rest of the terrestrials poured out of the hotel, Absu said, "Russell, my friend, bid your women to leave us. What I sorrowfully bring you is enough to challenge the eyes and stomach of a man."

John Howard was already shepherding the women away.

"There is a place where we have already buried one of our companions," said Russell, looking at Tore with difficulty. "I would be grateful, Absu, if we could take the body of our friend there, also. I think we shall want to lay him to rest in the earth as soon as possible."

Absu and the pathfinder dismounted. They followed Russell and John Howard to the place where Marina was buried, the pathfinder leading his pulpul with its sad and terrible burden.

The feathery seeds from the savanna were already piled

high over Marina's grave, with only the tip of the cross showing above the whitish, billowy mound. Russell found the exact spot with difficulty. He was thinking bleakly that perhaps the time had come to establish a formal cemetery.

Presently the small party was joined by Andrew Payne, who brought two spades. He had also brought a plain white sheet from the hotel. He spread the sheet out, and Tore was laid gently on it.

Absu said, "Lord Russell, this my servant, Farn zem Marur, discovered the body of your warrior. Greet him, that he may speak of it." Then he turned to the pathfinder. "Greet the lord Russell Grahame," he said solemnly. "Member of Parliament, Voice of the Queen's People, Creator of the Royal Laws, and one of great stature in his own land."

Farn zem Marur went down on his knees, took a poniard from inside his leather jerkin, placed the point on his breast, and offered the hilt to Russell. "Lord Russell Grahame, I am Farn zem Marur, pathfinder and warrior, if my life is required."

"Welcome," said Russell, at a loss. "You bring a sad burden, yet you are welcome." He held out his hand to take the hilt of the poniard and give it back to the pathfinder. He knew that Absu was very keen on formality and hoped that he was doing the right thing.

He wasn't.

"Do not touch the weapon," warned Absu, "unless you wish to kill him. He needs to know only that his life is not required."

"Stand, Farn zem Marur," said Russell, gravely. "Your life is not required."

The pathfinder stood up, a look of relief on his face. "Lord, I may speak?"

"You may speak."

"I discovered the body of your warrior, Lord Russell,

many varaks to the north of Keep Marur. I had been commanded by my sept lord to draw pictures of all the land wherein we now live, so that these pictures might again be drawn for you also. . . . Lord, I know not what to say of the death of your warrior. There was not the smell or mark of wild beasts about him. Nor yet were there wounds such as are received in battle. It may be that demons have made sport of him."

"The demons who did this work," said Russell grimly, "are such that I and my companions would wish to encounter."

"Well spoken," said Absu. "But a man cannot offer combat to demons, Russell. . . . If, however, these demons be of fleshy form, the lances of Keep Marur would joyfully demand of them a reckoning."

"Lord," said the pathfinder, "the body of this man was much plagued by flies and other small creatures when I found him. Therefore I formed the idea that he had died some time before. Though I looked for the agent of destruction, there was nothing to be seen. Yet he lay wedged between two rocks in such a manner that the task of loosing him was both difficult and one of little joy."

While the pathfinder had been talking, John Howard had steeled himself to examine Tore's body. He held something up and looked at Russell, pale and trembling.

"What do you make of that?"

Russell looked at the frayed and bloody wire. He saw where the strands seemed to enter into the half-severed waist. "That explains, at least, how he was almost cut in two," said Russell with difficulty. "Some bastard was probably dragging him along. He got wedged between the rocks, and whoever or whatever was on the other end of the wire just didn't want to know."

"Or wasn't equipped to know," said John with a sudden

intuitive flash. "Russell, the last time anybody saw Tore was that night when he told the girls he had an extra guard duty."

"But we know he didn't have one."

"Exactly. There was something he wanted to do, and it could only be done at night. . . . Three guesses?"

Andrew Payne shivered and felt the scar on his neck. "Spiders," he said.

"That's it! Tore was laying a trap for one of the spiders. . . . My guess is he wanted to follow one and see where it went. But in the dark he might lose it. So he found some way of attaching himself to the bloody thing."

Russell forced himself to bend down and look more closely at the remains. "The injuries could have been caused by him being dragged, I suppose. . . . Maybe he fell over and couldn't get up again. Or maybe the damned robot went far too fast for him, and he didn't get a chance to free himself."

"I think we've got it!"

"I think so, too. . . . Well, let's put poor Tore into the ground. There's nothing else we can do for him. I expect the others will want to say their good-byes to him, but we can leave that till tomorrow." He turned to Absu. "Allow us to lay our comrade to rest. It will ease our minds to bury him in the earth according to our custom. Afterwards, we will talk and offer you refreshment."

"Why do you not burn him?" asked Absu. "It is the custom in Gren Li to burn our dead. Thus are their spirits liberated into the air which gives them life."

"In our land also the dead are sometimes burned," replied Russell. "But here on this strange world we find it easier to bury."

"It is permitted that strangers be present?"

"We welcome your presence."

"Thus is our bond strengthened," said Absu simply. He watched Andrew start digging with a spade while John and Russell wrapped the body carefully in the plain white sheet. Then he glanced at the other spade and motioned to his pathfinder. "Farn zem Marur, we have brought a present of grief to this sept and the lord of this sept. Make deep the hole, that the friend of our friends and the grief of his death may be hidden from the sight of man forever."

18

The lord of sept Marur and his pathfinder, having left their weapons at the door as a token of trust, sat at a table in the bar of the Erewhon Hilton, gazing with some wonderment at the profusion of electric lights, and each sipping his first gin and tonic with proper respect. Eleven terrestrials were also present. Janice and Andrea—who had come to love Tore Norstedt and had cheerfully shared his attentions—had retired to weep their hearts out and console each other as well as they could.

Farn zem Marur unrolled a flayed and cured pulpul skin on the table before him. It was darker and rougher than parchment, but it served well enough for the little drawing and writing in which the Gren Li people indulged. On the pulpul skin Farn had drawn a pictorial map of the entire zoo. Keep Marur, Russell was amused to note, was a faithful representation of the original. The bridge huts of the People of the River were also accurately represented. But the Erewhon Hilton and its environs were shown by three concentric circles in which there was some minute writing that looked a little like Arabic.

"What does this mean?" asked Russell.

Absu smiled and sneezed. He was not yet used to the bubbles in the tonic water. "It means: Here live the magicians. For such you have proved yourselves to be."

Russell sighed. "Our skills, Absu, are limited. As you saw, they did not prevent our friend from dying."

"All men are mortal," returned Absu. "Even magicians.

Destiny knows no favorites. . . . What think you of the pathfinder's art?"

"I think he has made a very good map indeed." Russell turned to Farn. "You have yourself seen all that you have set down here?"

"Yes, Lord Russell Grahame. All that I have set down, I have seen. When I returned to Keep Marur, joyfully finding that my sept lord whom I had gone to seek had returned before me, I was again commanded to venture forth. The lord Absu required a full drawing of the land wherein we live, enclosed by vapors. This journey was long and not without hazard; for upon it I lost my pulpul and very nearly my life."

"How did this happen?" asked Russell.

"I was passing through the forest that lies near those who have their dwellings upon the river. I had stopped for a moment or two and had dismounted from the pulpul so that I might mark my progress upon the skin I carried with me. . . . Lord, it was well that I had dismounted, for no sooner had I done so than the pulpul fell dead, a rough lance having passed through it. By the robe, the thrust was a mighty one. But I had little time to marvel at it, for he who had hurled the lance presented himself with ax and war cry as my sword came free of the sheath. Matters seemed desperate, since the warrior, though poorly clad and armed, was great of stature and not without courage. It was fortunate that I have some little skill in the ways of disputation, otherwise my lord Absu might have experienced some displeasure with one who failed to return."

"You killed the stranger, then?"

The pathfinder smiled. "Lord Russell Grahame, in truth the warrior killed himself. He either cared nought for my weapon or was determined to perish. He ran upon my sword and was as amazed when it passed through him as I

was by the act. I know not which of us was the more
astounded. Then, even as he sank to his knees, with Death
lifting from him the need for argument, he spoke. And I
was again amazed that his tongue should be my tongue—as
it is so with you, Lord, and with the sept of magicians—
though the shapes his mouth made were strange and ugly."

"What did he say?" inquired Russell intently.

"Lord, the words were of the Gren Li language yet contained little substance. I could not understand."

Absu spoke sternly. "Pathfinder, do not neglect. The
lord Russell Grahame asks what he asks. Shake the dust of
memory and repeat the stranger's dying words. I command
it."

Farn zem Marur looked unhappy. "Lord, it was the nonsense of a dead man."

"Speak it, then, if you would avoid sharing his condition."

Farn zem Marur seemed most uncomfortable. Then he
said hesitantly: "Lord, the warrior spoke thus: Him-sharp-
thing-hard-sharp. Cold-hot. Bad-hurt-big-magic. You-man-
no-man. Him-thing-no-stone. Him-make-sleep-dark. Dark
dark-dark." The pathfinder shrugged apologetically. "Lord
Absu, I obey. The words were as I have said, but they were
uttered by a man with Death in his eyes."

"It is well," said Absu tranquilly, "that you have remembered."

There was a brief silence as all present contemplated the
strange word sequences uttered by the savage who had run
upon the pathfinder's sword.

Then John Howard said excitedly: "It fits, of course!
The People of the River have had the same kind of operation as we have. But, being primitive, their conceptual
thought is primitive. Hence the word strings and the foggy
description. . . . The poor devil had no experience of

metals, and even as he was dying he was still trying to find some description of what killed him. Within the limits of his culture, he was probably a very bright fellow."

"It reminds me of Bushman talk," said Paul Redman. "You know, the way the Australian aborigines link words together when they don't have any single word that will adequately say what they want to say. . . . When you come to think of it, these People of the River may be just about at the Bushman level of development."

"The matters of which your companions speak are doubtless of great interest," remarked Absu loftily. "But the People of the River, as you call them, Russell, are little more than animals of the forest. Besides the attack upon my pathfinder, they offered some indignity to a woman of the keep who was sufficiently foolish to venture far without escort. The woman is of no importance, but the insult to my sept is grave. Therefore, I propose to ride against these people. Their spirits may be great, but their numbers are no greater than ours. And I venture to think that few will tell their children of the lances of sept Marur."

"Absu," said Russell, choosing his words with care, "I know that you have cause for enmity with the People of the River, and I know that your code of honor is something of which you are justly proud. But I should be very sad if you destroy the People of the River before we have had a chance to offer them friendship."

"Friendship!" exploded Absu. "Friendship! Russell, I know that you magicians are a devious people. But even magicians do not offer friendship to wild animals. And such are these whom you would call men."

"Let me try to explain," said Russell patiently. "Let us suppose that no bond exists between you and me. Let us further suppose that I have insulted you. What would you do?"

"By the white queen and the black," retorted Absu, "I would resolve the argument most speedily with lance, sword, and poniard."

"But suppose," went on Russell, "that while we were fighting we became surrounded by wolves—that is, by animals who feed upon the flesh of men—what would you then do?"

Absu smiled. "The law of the robe makes provision for such a situation. You and I, Russell, would declare a truce until we had dispatched or driven away these creatures you have called wolves. Then we would resume our conversation."

"Well now," said Russell, "is it not possible that we are surrounded by wolves?"

"How so?"

Russell gestured to the pulpul skin on which the pathfinder had made his map. "We, you of Keep Marur, and, I believe, the People of the River, have all been abducted from our own worlds—I mean our own lands. We live now in a place that, as your pathfinder shows, is completely enclosed by a wall of mist. Our prison—for that is what we live in—is some sixty varaks wide, or, in our way of measuring, about forty kilometers. . . . Who knows, Absu, how we came here? Who knows whether or not we are surrounded by wolves? Until we can discover what lies beyond this mist wall, and whether we are surrounded by wolves or demons or fairies, I think it would be foolish indeed to risk reducing our numbers."

Absu sipped his gin and tonic thoughtfully. Again he sneezed. As he emptied his glass, Marion Redman brought him another. He accepted it without acknowledging her presence.

"You speak with a supple tongue, magician," he said coldly. "The wall cannot be penetrated, as you have learned. Therefore the land in which we live is the land that must be our home, until we are released by the Night Powers from this strange exile. This being so, I ride against the People of the River, knowing that, by bond law, you may not bar my path."

"I will not try to stop you, Absu. Indeed, if you can agree to my terms, I and some of my people will go with you. But first I must tell you that we magicians think we can find a way to pass through the wall of mist. We have also devised fearful weapons in case any should bar *our* path."

It took some time for Russell to explain how John Howard proposed to take temperature measurements in the river where it came through the mist wall and then by comparative tests taken downstream, together with measurements of the rate and flow, arrive at a rough estimation of the thickness and maximum coldness of the mist. But eventually Absu seemed to comprehend the project. The pathfinder, on the other hand, had grasped the principles involved very quickly. He and John Howard were poring over the map that had been drawn on the pulpul skin and were engrossed in the practical problems of setting up the experiment.

When Absu had finally grasped what it was all about, Russell took him to see the boat that Tore Norstedt had almost completed before he kept his fatal rendezvous with the spider robot. By now the sun had set, but the strip of road outside the Erewhon Hilton was illuminated by a string of electric lamps that had been rigged up as makeshift street lighting some days before.

Again Absu and his pathfinder marveled at the skills that enabled the magicians to produce light without flame. Night insects made dancing halos around the lamps, and the strip of roadway with the empty supermarket and the two useless cars, and with wisps of grass and dry leaves drifting along the deserted pavement, looked more than ever like a discarded film set.

While the rest of the terrestrials remained in the hotel considering the pathfinder's map, the way Tore Norstedt had died, and the discussion that had recently taken place, Russell, John Howard, Absu, and Farn zem Marur inspected the light, flat-bottomed craft that Tore had put together so carefully. It stood in one of the small workshops under the bright glare of a naked light bulb, with tools and strips of wood lying as Tore had left them. Looking at these signs of recent industry, Russell found it hard to believe that the young Swede would never come back to complete his task.

"The craft seems sturdy enough," conceded Absu. "We of sept Marur have little knowledge of the ways of traveling upon water, since our journeys are made upon land. But I do not doubt that your boat will be strong enough to pass down the river—if you are strong enough to pass through the mist. . . . What say you, pathfinder?"

"Lord Absu, the craft is strong, but the mist is cold. It may be that the price of passing through the mist is death."

Absu smiled thinly. "No doubt the magicians will know how to keep a man warm as he passes through the icy air of unbeing." He turned to Russell. "You spoke of fearful weapons, my friend. If indeed our prison is surrounded by wolves, such weapons may be needed. Show them to me."

John Howard brought one of his grenades—the gunpowder packed tight into a small bottle that had been bound with wire.

Absu held it in his hand. "Such as this does not look as if it will bring discouragement to either man or beast."

"Step outside, Absu," said Russell, "and do not be discountenanced by what you will see and hear. But when I ask you to fall down, do so with great speed."

When all four were clear of the buildings, John Howard lit the short fuse and hurled his grenade into the now dark savanna.

"Down!" shouted Russell. The four men fell flat on their faces.

Nothing happened for a moment or two, and Absu was just beginning to get up when there was a flash of light and the earth shook. The sound of the explosion was, to Russell, satisfyingly loud.

A look of awe came over Absu's face. He was speechless. Farn zem Marur still lay on the ground, covering his head with his hands and muttering incantations to ward off evil. It was, thought Russell, a historic moment—two medieval warriors getting their first experience of explosives.

"Truly," said Absu, when at last he was able to speak, "this is a weapon of much terror and destruction. By the robe, Russell, I am glad indeed that we entered the bond, you and I. A man may face metal with joy and courage; but from such a thunderbolt may he not turn away without great loss of honor."

"If he does not turn away," observed Russell grimly, "both he and his honor will rapidly perish. . . . Now it is late, Absu. You and your pathfinder shall rest with us this night. And I will explain why, though it would be easy to destroy the People of the River, we must ride against them not to kill but to take prisoners if we can."

19

The expedition against the People of the River, which took place some ten or twelve days after Absu mes Marur and his pathfinder had brought back the body of Tore Norstedt and had witnessed for the first time the tremendous power of explosives, was an unqualified success. No blood was spilled; and the People of the River were, in a sense, hoist with their own petard. Or, at least, two of them were.

Before the attack took place, a three-day reconnaissance was carried out by John Howard and Farn zem Marur. John showed the pathfinder how to use the binoculars; and between the two of them they managed to keep a more or less continuous watch. They verified the impression previously received by Paul Redman and his party that the primitive group was largely nocturnal in its habits. They also discovered that, whenever any of them left the bridge of huts to go into the forest on either side of the river, they always took the same routes. This enabled the attack to be carried out with an obvious and simple strategy.

It was timed to begin near to midday, when the People of the River would be most relaxed and—hopefully—most somnolent. It was to be carried out by six men only, divided into two forces. Russell and Andrew Payne were to be the "trigger mechanism"; and the force entrusted with the task of taking prisoners was to consist of John Howard, Farn zem Marur, and another Gren Li warrior, all under the command of Absu.

Tore's boat had been completed and had passed its fresh water trials very well indeed. The boat was a necessary part of the operation. It was to be used for carrying the long and bulky nets that it had taken the women of Keep Marur several days to make, and it was also to be used for ferrying Russell and Andrew with their two grenades across a broad stretch of river about two kilometers upstream from the bridge of huts.

On the day chosen for the operation Russell and John synchronized their watches. Then both parties set out shortly after dawn. Russell and Andrew began to paddle the boat, loaded with nets, downstream to the rendezvous point, while Absu, fully armed and accoutered and looking more than ever like a sunburned Mongolian St. George, led his small troop on pulpuls from the Erewhon Hilton, out across the savanna toward the southern forest.

Because the currents were a little faster than had been anticipated, Russell and Andrew arrived at the rendezvous shortly before Absu and his small party. But soon after the nets had been unloaded, the grenades checked, and their fuses fixed, Absu and his group arrived.

The plan was simply that Russell and Andrew, having got themselves to the other side of the river, would make their way unobserved to within fifty or sixty meters of the bridge of huts. By which time the reception party should be in position on the opposite bank.

When all was ready, Russell and Andrew, making as much noise as possible, would hurl their grenades near enough to the bridge of huts to create a spectacular explosion without—if possible—causing any actual damage. In theory, the People of the River ought to be so shaken by what, presumably, to them would seem like a manifestation of supernatural force that they would retreat—at speed, it was hoped—to the far side of the river, where Absu and his small company would be waiting for them.

Fortunately, practice and theory coincided.

The grenades not only made a very satisfactory double bang—as if the heavens were falling—but also flung large quantities of loose earth and stones into the air and, since the weather had been very dry, created a dust cloud that must have seemed to the occupants of the bridge of huts like the onset of darkness at noon.

It had been a warm, sunny morning, peaceful and relaxing. Then suddenly there were two terrible cracks of doom, followed by a hail of small stones and fragments of earth and a tremendous yelling. Under such circumstances civilized people might well have panicked. As it was, the People of the River were terrified.

Instinctively they ran away from the huts, away from the noise and the apparent source of destruction and straight into the line of nets that Absu and his three companions had suspended between trees along the customary route into the forest. If one of the net lengths had not refused to fall when its release rope was pulled, several of the Stone Age people might have been taken prisoner.

As it was, when Farn zem Marur and John Howard pulled their ropes, two of the People of the River, kicking and shouting, fell entangled to the ground. The rest, seeing strange creatures descend from the treetops, and no doubt utterly unnerved by the appearance of Absu, fully armored, with lance ready, and sitting tranquilly upon his pulpul, fled screaming into the forest. By the time they had recovered their wits, the attackers and their prisoners had departed, leaving behind them on the far side of the river two small craters as evidence of the magic forces that had been employed.

Since the prisoners had an apparently inexhaustible fund

of energy and refused to stay still or quiet even when they were bound and being sat on, Farn zem Marur sensibly knocked them both on the head. Then each was slung over the back of a pulpul for the return journey to the Erewhon Hilton. It was only when they were unconscious and being secured to the pulpuls that it was discovered that one of the prisoners was indisputably a woman. She was dressed in the same kind of rough animal skins as her companion, she had similarly long matted black hair, and her features —discernible because her face was a little cleaner—were only slightly softer. Her sex was proclaimed by full breasts that had burst out of her crudely sewn clothing during the struggles in the net.

Having secured their prisoners, the small party turned north and traveled as quickly as possible back through the forest. Absu would have preferred to stay and do battle if the surprised and dispirited enemy should recover themselves and regroup; but he had given his word to Russell that he would avoid taking life if possible. And whatever else he was, Absu mes Marur was a man of his word.

Meanwhile, Russell and Andrew had the harder task. Going downstream had been largely a matter of using the paddles to steer the boat. Taking it back upstream involved hard work for slow progress. It was nearly dark before they had moored the boat to the river bank at the point where it was nearest to the Erewhon Hilton.

By the time they had covered the few kilometers to the hotel, Absu and his party were already installed, and their prisoners, doubtless nursing considerable headaches, had returned to a mute and sullen consciousness.

20

If electric lighting, modern furniture, glassware, and twentieth-century clothing had astounded the people from a medieval culture, it completely terrified the two Stone Age people who now found themselves in surroundings totally beyond their comprehension. They had been taken into the lounge of the Erewhon Hilton, where they were being inspected by thirteen terrestrials and three warriors from Keep Marur.

Their hands and legs were still tied, but they had been arranged as comfortably as possible in two easy chairs. They were, perhaps, even more afraid of the chairs than of the other fantastic items with which they were surrounded. Possibly they suspected the chairs of being some kind of seats of sacrifice, or contrivances that would eventually swallow their victims whole.

Pathetically, they tried to draw close to each other and comfort each other. Interpreting their fruitless attempts correctly, Russell had the chairs placed side by side.

"I-not-run, you-not-run, I-you-see-not-hurt, not-cold-hurt," growled the man bravely.

"I-not-cold-hurt," whimpered the woman. "Cold-hurt-come. No-run, no-eat, no-touch-hold-close. Cold-hurt-come."

He tried to put his arm around her, remembered that he couldn't, then tried to lick her face. He couldn't make it. But he did manage to get his forehead onto her breast. The touch seemed to soothe her.

"No-cold-hurt-come," he mumbled without much conviction. "No-cold-hurt-come. I-you-laugh-eat. No-cold-hurt-come."

Russell had been listening and watching intently. It was easy enough to get into their way of speaking, because the thought processes were so simple. Cold-hurt obviously meant death.

"No-cold-hurt-come," he said experimentally. "You-she, no-cold-hurt-come."

The man jerked up, blinked, and snarled, baring his teeth like an animal. The woman whimpered.

"You-she stay still, rest," went on Russell soothingly. "No-hurt. You-eat, she-eat, no-hurt."

Again the man growled, but with less conviction. He looked hopelessly at the sea of faces surrounding him, then blinked once more at the electric lights and shivered.

"The poor bastard is absolutely shattered by it all," said Russell to no one in particular. "There are far too many of us, and the lights are hurting him. Have we got any candles? At least he will understand what a flame is."

"I too would like a simple flame better than the burning spheres," said Absu solemnly. "You magicians are enough to discountenance cultivated people, Russell, as well as these wretched brutes."

Marion Redman produced four candles, which were then lighted. At the same time Robert Hyman switched the electric lighting off, and the sudden change caused the two Stone Age people to rock and whimper, straining at their bonds. But after a moment or two they seemed to calm down.

"Absu, Anna, stay with me," said Russell. He turned to the others. "But I would be glad if the rest of you would go and have a drink or something. There will be time enough to inspect our captives, if we can manage not to frighten them to death."

"Lord Absu," said Farn zem Marur, "is it your wish that I and Grolig, your liegemen, should wait apart?"

Absu nodded. "Rest within calling distance, my children. I doubt that I shall need your blades."

"Russell, do you think we should fix some food for them?" asked Simone.

"Perhaps. . . . But it had better be simple stuff. Some kind of cooked meat, and plain water, I would imagine."

Presently, Absu, Anna and Russell were left alone with the prisoners.

"Not-hurt," said Russell. "We-you-not-hurt." He turned to Absu. "Cut the cord around the woman's hands, and let us see what she does."

When the man saw Absu take his poniard and approach the woman, he thrashed about like one demented. Russell made soothing noises to no avail. As Absu was cutting through the cords that bound the woman, her companion managed a curious jackknife kind of movement and succeeded in sinking his teeth into Absu's arm.

Absu dropped the poniard and with his free arm delivered a mighty flathand blow that must have rattled the teeth in the Stone Age captive's head. Then he picked the poniard up and finished sawing through the bonds.

The woman whimpered, looked at her mate, then began to stroke his head. Seeing that her arms were now free and that she had not been attacked, the man glared at his captors less malevolently.

"Not-hurt," repeated Russell. "We-you-not-hurt. Make-hands-move. Not-hurt."

Absu leaned over the Stone Age man and sawed away with his poniard. The man growled again but remained still until his arms were free. Then he suddenly grabbed the blade of the poniard, roared, let go, and gazed wonderingly at the blood on his hand.

"Christ!" said Russell. "It's going to be a long, hard night."

21

It was indeed a long, hard night but a rewarding one. For by the end of it they had established at least some simple communication with the captives and had inspired, perhaps, a small amount of confidence. By a laborious process Russell had managed to effect an exchange of names. The woman called herself Ora, and the man called himself Ireg.

Afterward, Russell realized that it was the exchange of names that brought about the psychological breakthrough. Up to that point Ora and Ireg had behaved as if every moment might be their last. They had gained a little confidence when freshly cooked meat was offered to them. They ate it greedily. But it had been a bad mistake to offer them water in glasses. Ora held hers wonderingly, not comprehending that it could be used for drinking.

Anna took the glass from her and demonstrated. Whereupon Ireg raised his glass to his mouth, took a great bite out of it, and spent the next few moments spitting out blood and slices of glass. Eventually a bowl of water was produced, and the captives scooped up handfuls eagerly, alternately sucking and lapping like cats.

One thing that Russell rapidly discovered was that Ora and Ireg were not unintelligent. They had an amazing capacity to learn. In a sense, thought Russell, they might be likened on the intellectual level to intelligent ten-year-olds who had been deprived of any education at all and allowed to run wild. He was reminded of stories he had heard long ago on Earth of children who had been lost in forests and had managed to survive.

But these were not children: They were mature adults, members of a small tribe in a primitive phase of development. Therefore, if it were possible to teach them, to increase their limited language to the point where it could cope with complicated thoughts, it might even be possible to lift them clean out of their Stone Age culture and perhaps introduce them to the rudiments of science and technology. What a fascinating project that would be!

But first there was the problem of communication. And as time passed, it became less formidable than Russell had feared. After the exchange of names, Absu cut through the cords that bound Ora's and Ireg's legs.

"Not-run," warned Russell. "You-she-walk, look, see things. Not run. You-eat, laugh, rest. Russell talk, Ora talk, Ireg talk. All talk."

Ora looked perplexed, but Ireg smiled. "You-good-thing-man," he said tentatively. "Russell-good-thing-man. Ireg-good-thing-man. Not-hurt."

Ireg stood up carefully and slowly, to show that he would neither run nor fight. Then he stretched himself, and the muscles rippled on his sturdy limbs.

Absu said solemnly: "You-big-thing-man. Hard-big. Hard-make-cold-hurt. Good."

Russell gazed at him in surprise.

"Do not be too surprised," said Absu dryly. "I, too, must learn to speak his strange word patterns, Russell. It may be that in the end Ireg and Absu mes Marur will understand each other well. Since each, in his fashion, is a warrior." He laughed. "I have thought much about you and your magicians, Russell. You once told me that you came from a world beyond the stars and on the far side of the sun. This I find hard to believe, since I know that the world is flat and that beyond the fire of the sun and the lanterns of the stars there can be nothing that a man may understand without first receiving the gift of madness—or, perhaps, of great wisdom. Yet I know also that you would not willingly deceive me and that many strange things have happened to bring all of us far from our own lands. It may be that Ireg and his kind have been brought here from a far country. Are we not all, then, brothers in misfortune? There is much that I must seek to understand."

Russell said: "Absu, my friend, I already knew that you were a brave man. Now I realize that you are a wise one."

Ora had stood up also and was now walking around the room examining large and small things wonderingly. She picked up a glass ashtray and made noises of childlike pleasure as she saw the candlelight shining through it. When she put it down again, very carefully, Anna took it and gave it to her.

"This-you-have. Keep," said Anna. "Anna-give-Ora-this-thing-keep. This-thing ashtray."

"Ora-keep-hold," said the woman smiling. "Keep-hold. Look-laugh. . . . Ashtray."

Ireg looked at the ashtray enviously. "Ireg-keep-hold," he said. "Thing-Ireg-keep-hold. Look-laugh."

Anna looked around. On a low table there was a small polished steel tray. She gave it to Ireg. He examined it with delight but let it drop with a crash when he glimpsed his own face reflected from its shiny surface.

Anna picked it up and gave it back to him. "Not-hurt," she said soothingly. "Ireg-keep-hold. Look-laugh. Not-hurt."

Suddenly Russell realized that he was desperately tired. No doubt the others were, too. Although Ora and Ireg were nocturnal creatures, they had had a very rough time during the last few hours. Their minds must be reeling under the impact of many frightening and apparently inexplicable experiences. He thought it would be a very good thing if everybody took a spell of rest.

But there were problems. He turned to Anna and Absu. "We are going to have to rest ourselves and them. But I don't think we can leave them alone. They may panic and wreck the place or try to escape and hurt themselves—or somebody else. I don't want to have to tie them up again." He grinned. "I think it would make them unhappy. So what should we do?"

"We can leave a guard," said Anna.

Russell thought about it, and shook his head. "They are just getting used to us. A guard—especially an armed guard —might provoke them."

"Then it is quite clear that we must all sleep in this place," said Absu. "Do not be uneasy, Russell. It is true that I am a little tired, having seen much of interest; but it is my custom to sleep lightly, as a warrior should. I doubt that our savage friends will be able to make any movement without Absu mes Marur noting it."

"I must confess that I came to the same conclusion," said Russell. "Let us hope that we can explain the idea to Ora and Ireg."

Ireg was now accustomed to his own reflection from the steel tray. Indeed, he seemed rather pleased by it and tried several ferocious and comic expressions upon himself. In the candlelight his hard, rather flat features had become softened so that, but for his coarse hair and clothing of animal skins, he might have passed—thought Russell—for one of the more unkempt specimens of twentieth-century manhood that frequented the King's Road in Chelsea. But, unlike the typical King's Road grotesque, there was much humanity in Ireg's eyes. Russell experienced a strange wave of sympathy for him—an innocent, catapulted by chance or design into a world he could never hope to understand.

"Ireg, you-sleep, Ora-sleep. Russell and Anna sleep. Absu sleep. Rest. Good-thing-do. Make happy."

"Sleep?" asked Ireg. "Sleep? How-sleep-you-show?"

Russell sat down in one of the easy chairs, closed his eyes, and tried to snore a little. "This-sleep. Make-good-strong. Make happy."

Ora laughed. "Warm-dark-good. Make warm-dark-good. Ora-Ireg lie-down-warm-dark."

"That is it," said Anna. "See Anna-sleep. Russell-sleep. Not-hurt. Warm-dark-good." She too leaned back in a chair.

The candles were burning low, and the room was full of warm, dancing shadows. Ireg tried a chair, then thought better of it. He took Ora's hand, and together they lay down on the carpet. Absu sat cross-legged a little distance away and allowed his head to droop.

But Ireg evidently had firm ideas about the proper preliminaries to sleep. After he and Ora had lain down for a while, his hand moved experimentally to her exposed breast. He took her left nipple between his fingers and tweaked it. Ora did not open her eyes, but her body responded. Thus encouraged, Ireg tweaked a little more. Ora still did not open her eyes, but she stretched luxuriously, and a strange gurgling noise seemed to come from the back of her throat.

Pretending to be sound asleep, Russell, Anna, and Absu mes Marur were aware of the entire operation. Ireg's love-play was crude but oddly tender. Presently, when Ora's body—she still did not open her eyes—seemed fluid and completely relaxed, Ireg flung himself upon her and made love in a strenuous and joyous fashion, completely oblivious of the watchers, who did their best to conceal their watching.

Ora rolled and writhed and pretended to fight now and

then but still did not open her eyes. She moaned a little and she laughed a little. Then presently the two Stone Age people fell fast asleep in each other's arms. Throughout the short but vigorous lovemaking neither had uttered a word.

Watching them surreptitiously through half-closed eyes, Russell thought that that was how it might have been in the Garden of Eden. He glanced at Anna and saw that she was looking at him. He wanted her. He had been excited by a couple of savages rutting, and he wanted her. She seemed to know all that was going through his mind, and he sensed that she too had been aroused.

But they did not make love. They just looked at each other. They did not make love because they were not alone.

And that, mused Russell sleepily, was probably the difference between innocence and experience. Ora and Ireg, bless them, did whatever they wanted whenever they wanted, oblivious of all else. They did not know about morals, or sophistication, or privacy.

They knew only about need. And, perhaps, about contentment.

And, quite possibly, that was really all there was to know. . . .

22

Ora and Ireg remained as "guests" at the Erewhon Hilton for six full days. Then they were taken back to the vicinity of the bridge of huts and released. During their captivity they made no attempt to escape. They were too busy learning. And during their stay Russell gave them a crash course in language development. They learned a lot of other things, as well; but without the development of language, their ability to grasp and store conceptual knowledge would have been very limited. So in the course of six days they were pushed into achieving a degree of intellectual progress that it had taken Stone Age man on Earth thousands of years to achieve. But of course the terrestrial Stone Age people did not have teachers.

Russell was amazed by the innate intelligence of the two primitive creatures. It surpassed his wildest hopes. Ora was particularly bright and would grasp a concept or the meaning of a new word long before Ireg. He, on the other hand, though slow, was more methodical. Once he had learned something, he could apply his new knowledge more efficiently than Ora.

By the third day conversation had become noticeably less arduous for all concerned. As vocabularies increased, the need to string words together in elaborate definitions grew less and less. Cold-hurt, for example, could be defined as death. Lie-hold-dark-close-laugh-cry could be defined as making love. And cold-hurt-no-hurt-eat-hurt could be called hunger.

Absu stayed long enough to see what the magicians were

doing with the two captives, then he returned to Keep Marur to attend to such domestic problems as beset a feudal lord. He left Farn zem Marur to hold a watching brief but took the other Gren Li warrior back with him. He told Russell that he would return in a few days to find out what progress had been made and to discuss the proposed attempt to pass through the wall of mist.

Meanwhile, Russell, Anna, John Howard, and the others pressed on with the education of Ora and Ireg. Farn zem Marur watched them with bright, intelligent eyes. He too was being educated; and he was learning more about the magicians than they would ever realize.

One afternoon Russell sat on the steps of the hotel— one of his favorite meditating places—with Ireg and the Gren Li pathfinder. Ora was somewhere inside the Erewhon Hilton being initiated by Andrea and Janice into the mysteries of modern feminine clothing and makeup. For the young British students the operation was a joke; but for Ora it was an explosive succession of miracles.

For a while the three men said nothing to each other. They had eaten well—Ireg, apparently, could dispose of any kind of food whatsoever—and were content with their own thoughts. The Gren Li pathfinder was idly using his poniard to carve a small fertility symbol which, as a mark of respect, he proposed to lay on the skins of the sept lord of the magicians. Ireg was practicing counting with ten small stones. And Russell was light-years away, indulging nostalgically in memories of the London rush hour on a foggy November afternoon.

Suddenly, Ireg said: "Russell-friend give words to Ireg. Ireg not give. Nothing give. Ireg wet-hurt, dark-down."

By this time, Russell was familiar enough with Ireg's way of talking to be able to pick up the nuances. He translated the statement as "You are teaching me, but I cannot teach you. I do not understand why you are teaching me, and I am sad that I have nothing to offer in return."

Russell thought about that for a moment, then he said, "Ireg give big thing to Russell-friend. Ireg give throw-stone hand." He held out his own hand expectantly.

With some wonderment Ireg cautiously held out the hand he used most for hunting or fighting. Solemnly Russell took it and shook it slowly. The hand, with its horny, calloused skin, felt more like the paw of some giant beast. When Ireg's fingers tightened, Russell winced with pain. Ireg noted and understood the gesture. He let go.

"Shake hand," said Russell, "means Ireg not hurt Russell, means Russell not hurt Ireg. Never never hurt. Because Ireg friend, Russell friend. Ora, all Ireg people friends. Anna, all Russell people friends. Never never hurt. This big thing Ireg give. . . ." Then, to emphasize it, he added, "Russell laugh, much happy, much good. Shake hand, warm hold, good big thing Russell Ireg make."

"Big thing," echoed Ireg, dimly comprehending. He could not understand why people who fought so terribly with loud noises, nets, ropes, and shiny things sharper than stones should not want to fight him and his people. But inscrutable are the ways of the gods. If this was what made these strange-smelling creatures happy, so be it. "Never never hurt. Big thing. Ireg people, Russell people, never never hurt." He brightened. "This Ireg give?" There was a questioning in his eyes.

"This Ireg give," affirmed Russell. "Good big thing. Bigger than words Russell give Ireg."

Ireg stood up and beat his chest. "Big thing Ireg give!" he shouted down the strip of empty street, as if trying to communicate with the savanna. "Never never hurt. Good big thing Ireg give!"

"Lord," said Farn zem Marur, looking up from his carving, "is it fitting that a sept lord should enter the bond with a savage?"

"It is fitting," said Russell evenly. Then he said, almost irrelevantly, "Am I a man or a beast?"

The pathfinder smiled. "You are lord of the sept of magicians."

"A man or a beast?" persisted Russell.

Farn zem Marur was disconcerted. "Lord, a man, I think —unless something greater."

"And you, Farn, and the lord Absu—are you men or beasts?"

Farn regained his composure. "For myself, I answer I am a man. . . . But my lord Absu casts a long shadow when weapons are drawn."

"Yet he is a man?"

"Much of a man."

"And Ireg, Farn. Is he a man, or is he a beast?"

Farn zem Marur cast an appreciative glance at the Stone Age man. "Lord, whether he is a beast with the heart of a man or a man with the heart of a beast, I know not. . . . Yet I think I would rather he were with me than against me. He has much strength and, in his fashion, some valor."

"I submit, pathfinder," said Russell, "that you and I and he belong to the class of beings we call men. Outside the barrier of mist which you know well, and which encloses us, there may be beings who are great in achievement yet are neither men nor beasts. The time may come when they may wish to dispose of us or when we may demand a reckoning."

"Lord," said Farn zem Marur, "in that case, we are all of one sept."

Russell grinned. "Take one step further, Farn zem Marur," he said. "In any case, we are all of one sept."

Ireg smiled down at them. "Good big thing," he announced sagely.

23

It was early in the afternoon, but though the sun was still high in a fleecy sky, there seemed to be an unusual touch of coldness in the air. Or perhaps it was not in the air, thought Russell, shivering slightly. Perhaps it was something inside him—the coldness of fear.

He looked at Anna, sitting by his side in the boat, paddling away with apparent unconcern. He thought she looked beautiful. He had not realized before just how beautiful she was. But then, he reflected, one takes so many things for granted until one is aware of the nearness of death.

Anna Markova's long dark hair was tied carelessly with a piece of string behind her head. She was wearing little but an open shirt and a pair of tattered trousers. All the warm clothing had been stacked neatly in the small, detachable, and now insulated cabin that Tore Norstedt had made before he died.

On top of the cabin, mounted neatly on a wooden rack, were three pairs of wooden wheels and two long shafts with a rope harness. These had been made by John Howard so that the boat could be converted into a miniature wagon for overland traveling. If indeed, thought Russell grimly, the need for traveling overland should ever be realized. For now that the journey of exploration had begun, his optimism had drained away; and he was convinced that it would end in disaster.

The cabin stood amidships—if that was not too grand a term—separating the bench on which Russell and Anna sat from the bench near the bow occupied by Farn zem Marur. Farn was adept at paddling Indian fashion; and his blade tirelessly chopped at the water on alternate sides. Fortunately, very little effort was required to keep the heavily laden boat moving, since it was traveling downstream. The paddles were useful chiefly to keep the boat clear of the banks and the occasional midstream obstacles. In places the lazily rippling ribbon of water was no more than seven or eight meters wide; but here and there it expanded into broad, slow-moving shallows. And there were times, even, despite the shallow draft of the boat, when it lightly scraped the bottom.

Looking at the sturdy shoulders and efficient movements of Farn zem Marur, Russell was glad that Absu had allowed his pathfinder to come on the journey. Absu himself had not volunteered because he believed that his first duty lay in looking after his sept. For this reason also he disapproved of Russell's taking part in the exploration. But he had kept his disapproval to himself, reflecting that the ways of the magicians were not as the ways of normal people.

Originally, Russell had wanted to bring Mohan das Gupta with him. But Anna had talked him out of the idea. If for any reason the expedition ended in disaster, she had pointed out, there would be a serious imbalance of the sexes at the Erewhon Hilton. Two men, Gunnar Rudefors and Tore Norstedt, had already died; and though Marina Jessop had committed suicide, the possible loss of another two men might eventually create complications that could destroy what was left of the small group—to say nothing of seriously weakening their defensive power.

Since Russell himself was determined to go—being convinced that, in the event of his nonreturn, John Howard as his official deputy would handle matters just as well, if not better—Anna maintained that she was the logical choice of companion. Certainly in many respects Anna Markova was as good and as practical as a man; but he realized that he had accepted her argument for purely selfish reasons. He had wanted her to come. Now, although he was still selfishly glad that they were together, he bitterly regretted his weakness. He would prefer to have her relatively safe with the others.

During his absence, however long that might be, Absu had promised to maintain regular contact with John Howard. In the event of trouble, they had agreed that the sept Marur would move into the Erewhon Hilton or the terrestrials into the Keep Marur as the situation dictated.

Russell did not have the slightest notion what kind of danger might necessitate such a joining up, but it had seemed a good idea to indulge in some contingency planning. After all, the entire situation was grotesque; and should one really be surprised if the nocturnal spider robots took it into their transistors to run amok, or if the "fairies" that had been seen but not contacted should suddenly descend on the occupants of the zoo with sinister intent?

He looked at Anna once more and saw that she was smiling at him. He put the fear behind him and returned her smile. Gloom could be infectious. What was needed was lighthearted confidence—gentlemen in England now abed, and all that rot.

Anna stopped paddling for a moment and kissed his ear. Then she whispered, "I am glad we are together, Russell, but I am still very much afraid. . . . Are you afraid, too?"

He wiped the sweat—cold sweat—from his forehead and touched her shoulder affectionately. "Do you really expect an old-fashioned Englishman to admit to an emancipated Russian woman that he's frightened?"

"If it is the truth."

"My dear," he said lightly. "You must allow me the privilege of a certain quaint hypocrisy. A gentleman never does his nut in the presence of a lady."

Anna laughed. "Already you make me feel better. It is strange, the effect of a few words."

"Strange indeed," agreed Russell. "You remember what it was like when we passed under the bridge of huts? Everyone was shouting and dancing about, and for a few terrible moments I thought Ireg and Ora had not managed to persuade the People of the River that we were friendly —or else that Ireg had decided he could get along quite well without friendship."

"It was terrifying," said Anna. "It seems so long ago, but I suppose it is only about three or four hours."

"Less, I think," said Russell. "I was beginning to believe we would end up in a Stone Age cooking pot, especially when Ireg pushed off from the bank in his dugout canoe and came at us jabbering away and brandishing his best hunting ax."

Anna smiled. "All he did was throw it into the boat."

"That was the point. Do you remember what he said? He said: 'Ireg give Russell-friend good big thing. Stone little thing but carry good big thing. Hold hard, Russell-friend. Go quick. Come quick. Then Ireg-friend Russell-friend laugh hurt, eat hurt.'"

Anna started to paddle once more. "That was a big speech for Ireg. Perhaps the biggest he has ever made."

Russell picked up the stone ax from the bottom of the boat and held it wonderingly. "I don't really know why," he said, "but it made me feel rather proud. . . . I suppose it is something to have established friendship with a man like Ireg."

The boat had reached a broad patch of the river. The banks were low and sandy; and on either side the green, treeless plain stretched far into the distance. The character of the country had changed. The high savanna grass and the patches of forest had been left behind. The short, smooth grasses that covered the land seemed so even that they might recently have been cut.

Far away, Russell spied a herd of grazing animals. He took the binoculars out of the cabin and inspected them more closely. But for the single horns set centrally on their heads, it would have been easy to mistake them for young domestic bulls. It occurred to him then that he had really seen very little of the indigenous wild life—if, indeed, these creatures were indigenous—on the world that had come to be called Erewhon. Apart from the pulpuls imported for the benefit of the occupants of Keep Marur, the wild creatures seemed to be concentrated in the forests near the camp of the People of the River. But perhaps even those creatures had been imported for the benefit of Ireg and company, who were natural hunters. So quite possibly these creatures grazing in the distance might have been brought for the benefit of yet another group.

There were so many questions to be answered. So many curious occurrences to be explained. So much to know! Absently, Russell stroked the small bump on the back of his head—all that remained of the miraculous operation that presumably enabled everyone to communicate with one another directly.

Strange, too, how everyone was adapting to their new environments and learning to accept the miraculous, the crazy, the grotesque, and the absurd. Perhaps it all really was some strange, prolonged dream. Perhaps Anna, apparently real and living in the day and deliciously warm and exciting at night, was no more than a vivid projection of his mind—an illusion of life, breathing and pulsing nowhere except in his sleeping brain. Perhaps Absu, Keep

Marur, pulpuls, Stone Age people, spider robots, and all were fantasies—figments of an insane or a dying dream. Perhaps the jet from Stockholm to London had crashed and even now Russell Grahame, M.P., was under the surgeon's knife, hanging between life and death, shielded from the pain of the scalpel by anesthetics and a nightmare of his own creation. Perhaps . . .

"Lord Russell," said Farn zem Marur, breaking the reverie, "I think that we are no more than a few varaks—perhaps eight or nine—from the wall of mist. Would it not be well to rest, to eat, and to refresh ourselves before we hazard our bodies against the coldness of the barrier?"

"A wise thought, pathfinder. Let us pull into the bank and prepare ourselves. We must also take the warm clothing out of the cabin and have it ready to put on."

As he spoke, Russell thought of the comparative temperature readings that John Howard had made a few days before, far to the north. According to John's calculations, the mist barrier was probably no more than fifty meters thick. But the calculations, as John had pointed out, were no more than flimsy guesswork, since there was no means of knowing how low the temperature of the mist fell in its center. For reasons which Russell could not clearly understand, John had worked on the assumption that the temperature would not fall more than fifty degrees below zero. On that basis he estimated that the heat reduction of the river as it emerged from the mist barrier into the zoo indicated a minimum thickness of thirty meters and a maximum thickness of about fifty. But he could be wrong, terribly wrong. And if he were, there would soon be three hard-frozen bodies as the price of his error.

While Farn zem Marur steered the small boat in toward the left-hand bank of the river, Russell looked through his binoculars once more across the treeless plain. There in the distance, to the planetary south, a curved white wall seemed to rise up to merge in places with low-lying cloud. It was difficult to estimate the height, but Russell guessed that the mist barrier must be at least two hundred meters and perhaps even as much as four hundred meters high.

If it were so high, it was unlikely that the wall of mist would be only fifty meters in thickness. His heart sank, and the coldness inside him became more intense.

He did not point out the mist barrier to Anna and Farn zem Marur. He did not need to. Even without the binoculars they had already noticed the distant white wall that marked the boundary of their prison.

24

The river remained broad. At a distance of half a kilometer the mist barrier hung formidable and motionless across it like a great white cliff of ice. It was truly awe-inspiring. Because the river was wide, there was less chance of the boat's lodging against the banks with its three frozen occupants remaining frozen until the wall of mist was dispersed—if ever. But, also because the river was now wide, it was dangerously shallow; and consequently the risk of running aground was increased.

Russell surveyed the great barrier and felt rivulets of sweat running down his body. He was cold inside, but his body was drenched with perspiration. He was wearing two shirts, three sweaters, two pairs of trousers, and three pairs of socks and held in his hand a long woollen scarf which he presently intended to wind around his head.

Anna and Farn zem Marur were similarly muffled. Looking at them, Russell was incongruously reminded of a Christmas game he had played long ago as a child. He could not remember the details, but it involved being dressed in a great variety of old clothes and trying to eat a bar of chocolate with a knife and fork while somebody threw dice for a double six.

He laughed at the memory. Farn and Anna gazed at him in amazement.

"Lord Russell," said Farn, "it seems to me that there is little for laughter in yonder prospect. The cold is such that I have not known its like before. Nor, if we pass through the mist and live, shall I be eager to know its like again."

"I am sorry, Farn," said Russell contritely. "I was reminded by our clothing of a game that I once played as a child. . . . Is the cabin free of all our belongings?"

"Lord, I have placed everything at the head of the boat, as you ordered."

"It is well. The cabin will scarce hold the three of us, even when it is cleared." He gazed at the small pile of equipment that Farn zem Marur had stowed methodically.

The weapons were all piled together—the pathfinder's sword, poniard, and short spear, the knives, the two arbalests with their quivers of bolts, and the gunpowder grenades that belonged to Anna and Russell. By the weapons lay the boxes of canned foods and the bottles of hotel water that Anna and Russell drank in preference to river water. There were also the binoculars, Farn zem Marur's lodestone, two coils of rope, a box of makeshift bandages, and the instant picture camera.

What an odd collection of equipment, thought Russell. To mount an expedition like this with two men, one woman, and such a sorry heap of possessions one must surely be half crazy, half in love with death, or both. Even assuming they passed safely through the mist barrier—and that was a very big assumption—there was no knowing what lay on the other side.

Suppose the zoo, prison, or whatever had been conceived as a refuge or reservation in a wilderness of predatory beasts? Suppose there were nothing but featureless desert? Suppose the spider robots, or some other type of watchdog, had orders to destroy all who attempted to escape. Suppose, suppose, suppose . . .

"Russell, hold me," said Anna, looking like a fat rag doll. "Hold me close, very close."

Russell gazed at the great wall of mist, now no more than

a hundred meters away. He fancied he could already feel its coldness striking his face.

"I'll hold you when we get in the cabin," he said. "I'll hold you as tight as you wish." He turned to Farn zem Marur. "Pathfinder, these are my orders. When I give the word we will all crawl into the cabin, lying very close together, covering our heads and using our own breath to stay warm. If, as I hope, we should remain conscious during the penetration of the mist, and if the boat should run aground because the water is very shallow, we shall first attempt to dislodge it by rocking our bodies. If that should fail, you will crawl out of the cabin and try to move it with a paddle. But you must not open your eyes. If you cannot move it alone, I will join you in the effort. If the two of us cannot move it, the lady Anna will help us. And if the three of us cannot move it, the journey is at an end."

"Lord," said the pathfinder. "You have spoken. I am content."

The great white wall was now only twenty meters away. In the bright sunlight it was dazzling, hypnotic. But the sheer weight of its coldness was already apparent.

With a last glance, Russell assured himself that the boat was in midstream on a straight course. The rest was in the lap of the gods.

"Now," he said, "let us crawl into the cabin. The lady Anna shall lie between us. . . . And press close, Farn zem Marur, for in this there can be no disrespect." He kissed Anna lightly on the lips. "You first, love. Go and get yourself comfortable. And for God's sake keep your nightdress or whatever it is well over your head." Then he added flippantly, "And don't mind if two gentlemen become a trifle familiar."

"I think I love you," said Anna simply.

"I should hope so. This is no time for an estrangement."
He watched her crawl into the cabin, then he motioned to
Farn zem Marur.

"Lord Russell," said the pathfinder, "let us hope that
this shall be a story for our children's children. Whatever
befalls, know that I am honored by your presence."

"Get along with you, ruffian. We shall live to toast each
other under the table." Russell's voice was light even as the
mist closed about him and the first ice crystals formed on
his lips.

The boat had already drifted inside the opaque white
wall as he scrambled after Farn into the cabin and held the
shapeless bundle that was Anna in a viselike grip.

25

The coldness bit into them. It was like a great blind animal striking at them with myriad needle-sharp teeth of oblivion. It was like fire and death.

Their heads were covered, their eyes were closed, their bodies rigid with the sudden, terrible attack. Ice crystals formed on their faces; tears froze before they could be shed, welding eyelids and eyelashes together with a bond that seemed harder than steel. The moisture in their nostrils began to freeze, thinning down the air intake that struck in their heaving lungs like twin knives.

It would be a photo finish, thought Russell dully. If the cold itself did not kill them first, they would die of suffocation as their noses and mouths froze solid. He tried to hold Anna even tighter, but his muscles would not respond. Her head was close to his, and he fancied he heard a low deep groan forced from her immobile body. He wished briefly that he could see her face. Then he was glad that he could not.

Somewhere there was a dull grinding noise. No doubt the surface of the river in the heart of the mist was a solid sheet of ice, with the warmer currents flowing underneath it. If that were the case, the small boat would be wedged into it for ever. He should have thought of that possibility before the expedition started. He should have thought of so many things.

He should have thought that, whatever mysteries surrounded them, life was still sweet with Anna and the rest. He should have thought that perhaps there were some things it was better not to know—and certainly some things that were better not attempted. Such as crazily trying to break through a barrier that had been created by superior beings with a demonstrably superior science for the plain purpose of keeping their prisoners in.

He was getting drowsy, and his thoughts were becoming confused, and the pain was lessening as sensation was frozen out of his body. And it seemed that the very images in his head were freezing solid, and there was nothing left to do now but sleep coldly for ever.

He wished sleepily that he could have spoken to Anna, so near him in the darkness and yet so far away in her own shrunken universe of suffering. He wished very much that he could have spoken to her. Yet what was there to say?

I'm sorry, my love, he thought desperately. I'm sorry I got you into . . .

And then there was no thinking left.

Only an icy, timeless limbo . . .

Abruptly, the heavens cracked, the miracle happened, the world—or was it yet another world?—was shrieking with color and warmth and scents and sound. The return to consciousness, the dizzy riot of sensation, exploded upon him like a bomb.

He opened his eyes, screamed with pain, closed them again, and opened them again. He saw Anna's face above him, and beyond, the blue backcloth of the sky. Experimentally, he tried to move his fingers. They moved. He tried to move his arm. It also moved, but with a strange and immense stiffness. He sat up and began to laugh. Then he realized that the laughter was hysterical and fought it down.

"We're alive," he said wonderingly.

"Yes, Russell, we are alive. Now just rest a little while I see what I can do for Farn. He came out of it worse than either of us, I fear."

Presently Farn zem Marur was sitting up, no doubt experiencing the same fantastic sensations of returning consciousness that had afflicted Russell.

Russell gazed around him. He was leaning against one of the benches. Anna, remarkable woman that she was, must have dragged both him and Farn out of the cabin. He was amazed at her stamina and endurance.

The boat had drifted—or had been guided—into the bank. Upstream, about two hundred meters away, the mist barrier rose, curving away in a uniform arc across the land on either side of the river. It seemed even more formidable now that they had passed through it and lived. Russell shuddered at the thought that, according to the original plan, they would eventually have to trundle the boat, disguised as a wagon, around the great perimeter of mist and reenter their prison where the river entered it in the north.

Spluttering, and mouthing gratitude and incantations to the robe, the white queen and the black, and other Gren Li solemnities of which Russell had not previously heard, Farn zem Marur had returned noisily to the land of the living.

Russell was still puzzled by Anna's ability to recover faster than either he or Farn had done.

"If you are representative of Soviet womanhood," he said with a grin, "Russia is destined to dominate the Earth. Perhaps it's as well I shan't be there to see it. . . . How did you recover so quickly, Anna? Did you have a secret weapon?"

She nodded. "Chivalry, my love. I was chivalrously squashed between two men who felt it was their duty to protect the weaker sex. You were both very good insulators." She smiled impishly. "Also, though you may not have noticed it, I am more richly endowed with fat than either of you."

"Praise be to St. Lenin and Mother Russia for favors gratefully received," he retorted piously.

"Lord," said Farn zem Marur. "We who were as dead are now living. Truly there is much wonder in this thing. Our children's children may yet hear the story with some interest."

"Amen to that," said Russell. "And now that we have escaped from our prison, we had better try to find out what kind of world we have entered. One thing seems sure: There must be many strange things on this side of the mist barrier that are not on the other side. Otherwise there can be little reason for its existence."

It was at that moment, as he glanced casually at the surrounding countryside—which superficially seemed similar to the land on the other side of the barrier—that Russell noticed the column. It was in the distance, perhaps ten kilometers away; and he noticed it chiefly because late sunlight, reflected from its surface, made it seem like a slender, shimmering finger of flame.

The column was obviously very high. On top of it there was something that looked like a great green translucent bubble.

Russell gazed at it for a moment, spellbound. Then, rubbing his eyes, he groped for the binoculars.

26

It was now very late in the afternoon; and it would not be long before the sun sank over the western plain and left the world of Erewhon to twilight and then darkness. After their recent traumatic experience in passing through the wall of mist, and also because the day was nearly over, Russell judged it unwise to attempt to explore further until the three of them had rested properly. In any case, to travel across unknown country in darkness would be to invite trouble. So during what was left of daylight they hauled the boat ashore, took all their equipment out of it, and fitted two sets of wheels and the harness so that they would be ready for an early start on the following morning.

When darkness fell, Russell proposed that two people should sleep in the boat that was now a wagon, while the third remained to watch. If no one turned in until fairly late—and there was still a meal to prepare and dispose of, as well as other small tasks—a two-hour watch from each person should see them through until daybreak.

Before he engaged in setting up camp, Russell made what use he could of the remaining light to inspect their immediate environment and to look at the enigmatic column through his binoculars. The land nearby was smooth, almost featureless, and offered little concealment to wild animals or to any other beings. Indeed, no wildlife was visible on either bank of the river; and as far as that aspect was concerned, it looked as if they had been fortunate enough to find an ideal camping ground.

Through the binoculars the column and its translucent bubble were even more tantalizing and inscrutable than to the naked eye. The binoculars had a magnification factor of twelve, so they made the column look as it might appear if it were, perhaps, only a kilometer away.

Russell estimated its height at about seven hundred or eight hundred meters—then he dismissed the thought as plainly ridiculous. On that basis the green translucent bubble would be at least a hundred and fifty meters in diameter. Surely such a tremendous construction was beyond the bounds of reason?

But then, was not everything they had experienced so far on this nonsensical world of Erewhon beyond the bounds of reason? So why should there not be an entire forest of one-hundred-and-fifty-meter diameter bubbles poised on top of eight-hundred-meter stalks?

So far as he could discern, the column was metallic, circular, and featureless. But at that distance the binoculars could not resolve any surface decoration or markings unless they were very large. Around the base of the column there seemed to be a cluster of buildings; but they could easily be large rock formations, and it was impossible to make them out clearly in the fading light.

The bubble itself was the most baffling part of the whole ensemble. It was perfectly spherical in shape; and Russell saw—or thought that he saw—right through it, discerning the vague shapes of cloud formations apparently on the far side. But whether it was transparent or not, it was certainly translucent, being penetrated by shafts of light from the setting sun. It seemed, above all, curiously light and insubstantial—as if a sudden gust of wind might carry it away, or as if it might pop and be gone for ever with the abrupt transience of a soap bubble.

By the time darkness came, the air had turned cool; and the three explorers had to put on again some of the extra clothing they had worn to penetrate the mist barrier. There was also the question of a meal, since none of them had eaten for several hours. Besides the supply of canned food, the boat had been stocked with several bundles of small pieces of wood, primarily intended for kindling. But as there were no trees nearby from which wood could be obtained to sustain a large fire, Russell decided to use two or three bundles of kindling to heat the evening meal and to cheer them up.

The meal was a simple one, consisting mainly of beans and soup. It was eaten for the most part in silence. But when it was over, Russell began to talk of the strategy of exploration. It was obvious that for the return journey they would have to trek around the wall of mist and reenter their prison where the river entered it in the north. This in itself would be quite a task, since Farn zem Marur had estimated the distance between the river's point of entry and its point of exit at about fifty varaks, or thirty-five kilometers. Allowing for the curvature of the mist wall, this meant that the boat/wagon would have to be hauled about forty-five kilometers across unknown terrain before it could be launched once more.

And this could only be done in that distance if the exploration party kept fairly close to the mist barrier, which in turn would greatly limit their investigation. The fact that a curious and immense structure had already been seen in the distance—clearly the work of intelligent and technologically advanced creatures—prompted Russell to suggest an alternative plan.

"If we have to take the boat with us wherever we go," he said, "We shall find it very difficult to do any worthwhile exploration before we run out of food and energy. I think that it might be better to leave it near here, carry out perhaps two days' investigation, then take the boat north, keeping close to the mist all the way. At least we know that there is something worth looking at near here. . . . What do you think, Farn?"

"Lord, the great tower we have seen is truly wonderful. If, having already encountered some peril to make this journey, we cannot face a little more peril, I think that our effort will have been in vain. We came to learn, therefore let us learn, though the price of knowledge may be high."

"Well said. . . . And you, Anna? What do you feel? If we leave the boat, there is a chance that it may be destroyed. If we take it with us, we will have to keep close to the mist and our progress will be slow."

"I agree with you and Farn. We have taken risks to come this far. I am willing to take a few more to satisfy curiosity. . . . I think the tower is part of a city. If that is so, at least we should come face to face with our captors at last" —she laughed—"even if they do pop us into the cooking pot. It is so frustrating being a prisoner and not knowing why one is a prisoner or who holds the keys of the prison."

"Well, that is settled, then. In the morning we will try to find some inconspicuous place to leave the boat. Then we will take what provisions and weapons we can carry comfortably and have a closer look at the beanstalk."

"The beanstalk?" Farn zem Marur was puzzled.

"In my country," explained Russell, "there is a children's story about a very high bean plant on top of which there lived a most ferocious giant." He saw the look of alarm on Farn zem Marur's face and added hastily, "Not that I think that the green bubble will contain any giants. Perhaps it is simply some great machine for collecting or radiating energy. . . . I am sorry, Farn. Forgive me. I speak of things which you cannot understand."

"Lord, there is nothing to forgive. I am proud only that a great magician should not disdain the company of a humble Gren Li pathfinder on a journey such as this. I have already learned much, and I do not doubt, with the grace of the robe, that I shall learn more."

The small fire that had been used to heat the food was already dying. In the clear sky above, the profusion of stars—alien constellations which were already becoming familiar in their very strangeness—betokened a cold night.

"Farn," said Russell, "it is time that we rested. The lady Anna will take the first watch. I will relieve her, then you will relieve me, taking the last watch until dawn."

"Do you think I should be armed, Russell?" asked Anna half-jokingly.

"Yes. You'd better have a crossbow and one of the grenades. . . . But if we have any bad-tempered visitors, love, for God's sake don't start anything that we can't finish."

Presently, with Farn zem Marur and Russell resting in the cabin of the boat, Anna Markova began her quiet vigil. The air, though abnormally cold, was still; and there was nothing in the sounds of the night to cause her any anxiety. Occasionally she made short patrols. Occasionally she peered through the darkness in the direction of the tower, fancying that she could see its immense shape. Once, toward the end of her watch, she thought she saw an intense flash of green light. But almost before her eyes had registered it, the landscape was in darkness once more.

Presently she handed over to Russell, who in turn roused Farn zem Marur about two and a half hours before daylight. The night had been quite uneventful. The three of them might have been entirely alone on this strange planet.

27

The city—if, indeed, it was such and not some kind of scientific station—was small and strange beyond imagining. It was deserted. It was like a ghost town—and yet there was an air of cleanness and use and the subtle impression of recent occupation. It had, above all, the mood of a place that was waiting for something to happen. That something would happen—something fantastic, or beautiful, or terrible—Russell had no doubt. The signs all pointed to it. All three of the explorers had the uneasy sensation of being watched; and, in fact, all three knew that their progress toward the great column had been watched.

The column was even taller, more impressive, and more inexplicable than he had expected. It stood at the center of the city/ghost town/scientific station, rising almost a kilometer into the sky, supporting the vast, shimmering green bubble like some monstrous flower on a rigid metal stem.

As he stood gazing at it in awe, the events of the morning flashed rapidly through Russell's mind, convincing him more than ever that he, Anna, and Farn zem Marur were the principal actors (or victims?) of a drama that would shortly unfold.

Shortly after daybreak they had breakfasted and then looked for a suitable place to leave the boat/wagon. They found it a few hundred meters downstream, where there was a small gully sufficiently deep to conceal the boat from curious eyes. With the harness over his shoulders, Farn zem Marur hauled the boat to its hiding place. Then he and Russell lowered it carefully down the side of the gully. From ten paces away it was impossible to see, and even from the river it would have been very difficult to pick out.

They chose the food and equipment to take with them very carefully. It would be folly to weigh themselves down, but it would also be stupid to travel without enough food or adequate defense. With sad hindsight, Russell realized that they should have brought rucksacks or even suitcases —of which there were several at the Erewhon Hilton. But, according to the original concept of the journey, they would have been taking the boat with them wherever they went. As it was, they had to make rough bundles out of blankets. Besides an assortment of clothing, Farn zem Marur carried his sword and poniard and a food bundle. Anna carried her crossbow and a supply of water in bottles wrapped carefully so that they would not smash against each other. And Russell carried his own crossbow, two grenades, a coil of rope, the binoculars, and a can or two of food in his pockets.

The morning was a fine one, with the sun shining steadily and warmly from a blue sky. When they were ready to move, the small party headed directly toward the high column, which in bright sunlight seemed even more curious than on the previous day and somehow oddly alive.

Russell glimpsed the first sign of movement less than half an hour after the journey across the grassy plain had begun. He had formed a habit of stopping every few minutes to survey the landscape through his binoculars; and on one of these occasions he had noticed an irregular flashing two or three kilometers away, as of sunlight on something shiny.

He gave Anna the binoculars. Presently she handed them to Farn. Whatever was causing the flashes was making its way at a fairly high speed toward the river and the wall of mist. With this interesting discovery, Russell judged it wise to take a short rest. The three of them lay down on the grass so that they could see without being seen.

But their progress apparently had already been noticed. The flashes became larger and seemed now to be coming directly toward them. Farn zem Marur gripped his sword expectantly, Anna fitted a bolt to her crossbow, and Russell held his gas lighter and one of the gunpowder grenades.

Presently the flashing was identified. It was caused by a small troop of spider robots, the sunlight dancing on the metal spheres that housed their sensing and control mechanisms.

This was the first time that Russell and Anna had seen the spider robots in action and in daylight. It was the first time that Farn zem Marur had seen them at all. But the pathfinder, Russell was relieved to note, did not panic—not even when the spider robots were within fifty paces.

"We might as well stand up now," said Russell. "They know we are here. . . . If they have any orders or instructions concerning us, we shall soon find out."

"Lord," said Farn zem Marur grimly, "a sword is perhaps not the best of weapons to combat creatures such as these."

Russell glanced at the grenade. "No, pathfinder, but this may help. If the robots attempt to harm us, some will need a few spare parts afterward."

There were five of the spider robots, and each of them was carrying a box with the four multijointed appendages it used as arms. The boxes appeared to contain provisions that were probably destined for the Erewhon Hilton. The five robots came to within twenty paces of the three humans, halted for a moment, then abruptly turned away, almost as if they had just received further instructions. Russell watched them scuttling urgently toward the mist barrier, which now lay more than two kilometers behind, looking in the sunlight like a wall of solid ice. He wondered if the robots would simply march straight through the freezing barrier or whether there was a special place for entry and exit. It would have been useful to find out; but even if he had wished to backtrack and follow the robots, it would have been impossible to keep their pace. He picked up his crossbow and the coil of rope and signed to the others to continue the journey. Suddenly he was aware of the sweat dripping down his face and realized that he had been very much afraid.

He looked at Anna and Farn, perversely pleased to note the traces of fear evident on their drawn faces and still in their eyes. "If one senses danger," he said, "it becomes harder to bear when nothing happens." He laughed. "At least it seems that we are not to be punished prematurely for breaking out of prison. . . . So let us get to that tower and try to find out what it is all about."

They resumed their march in silence, each preoccupied with private doubts and anxieties. Every now and again Anna came and held Russell's hand for a few moments, as if she were reassuring herself of his actual presence or as if she were able to draw some consolation or strength from mere contact.

By Russell's calculations they had just about completed the first half of the journey from the river to the column when they saw the "fairies." Although no more detail of the column or the green bubble was apparent than when they had originally seen it, its sheer size, its utter domination of the surrounding landscape both oppressed and excited them. It was possible to discern, also, that the structures around its base were buildings of some kind; and this gave Russell added reason to hope/fear that at last they would encounter some of the race that had been responsible for their abduction from worlds far away.

It was Farn zem Marur who noticed the "fairies"—he thought of them as demons—first. He was too horrified to speak and could only point with a shaking hand.

The "fairies"—perhaps nine or ten of them—were flying swiftly through the air at an altitude of about one hundred meters. They seemed to be heading toward the green bubble, and they seemed to be responsible for a curious kind of low, even humming that reminded Russell of the sound made by a musical spinning top he had once possessed long ago in the bright world of childhood.

But there was hardly time to form any impression at all; for suddenly the "fairies" vanished. In midflight they seemed to wink out of existence as if someone somewhere had just thrown a switch and abolished them.

Russell rubbed his eyes, blinked, and felt his knees become unsteady. He regretted bitterly that no brandy had been included in the stores.

"You saw them?" He turned to Anna. But before she could reply, he already knew the answer.

"I saw them." Her voice was shaking. "I saw them. . . . Russell, Russell, I want to go back." Her voice rose in pitch and intensity. "Please take me back to our friends. Please, *please* take me back! If we go any further, we are all going to go mad. . . . We shall die, and then—"

He slapped her, and the hysterical torrent of words was cut off. Anna pulled herself together. "Thank you," she said simply. When she had calmed down a little, she said with a faint smile, "I am reminded that a Russian woman is, after all, only a woman."

"I didn't hurt you?"

"Only enough."

Russell turned to Farn zem Marur. "Pathfinder, we have

seen what we have seen. Is it your wish to go forward and perhaps encounter yet stranger things?"

Farn zem Marur's voice was none too steady. "It is my wish and my duty to follow the lord Russell Grahame, that I may not be dishonored in the eyes of my sept lord and in my own eyes."

"Let us go then. The answer to such mysteries as we have seen may lie ahead."

"Lord, they were not demons?"

"No, Farn, they were not demons."

"Nor were they fairies," said Anna. "I was reminded of something. . . . I was reminded of large dragonflies. . . . Perhaps they are only some kind of great insect."

"Insects which can disappear at will," said Russell dryly. "I can see why Paul Redman thought they were fairies, though—the brilliant wings, the golden hair . . ."

Anna laughed somewhat unsteadily. "They were not fairies. They had no wands. Only, I think, four legs."

Presently, when the sun was high in the sky, they came to the first group of buildings, which lay no more than a kilometer from the base of the great column. The buildings were low, windowless, igloo-shaped, and constructed of what appeared to be a plastic similar to that of the "coffin" from which Russell had emerged on his first day on Erewhon.

Cautiously the explorers approached the nearest building. They were aware of a kind of muted throbbing, such as might emanate from very powerful engines. They felt the vibrations first through the soles of their feet; but as they came closer it seemed as if the air around them were somehow charged with great pulses of energy.

Even if they had wanted to—and they were not entirely eager—they were unable to investigate the source of the throbbing further. For what were clearly the entrances to the buildings, squat tunnel-like protrusions about a meter high and a meter wide, were closed. The doors were made of metal, and there was no visible means of opening them.

The next group of buildings, similar in shape and size, were, however, open to inspection. Leaving his companions outside, Russell entered the first one and found that it contained stores of some kind—long, low racks on which were neatly stacked metal, plastic, and ceramic objects. Some of them looked as if they might be machine parts, while others looked like vessels of some kind. He stared at the long racks and was no wiser.

But in the second building, whose door was open, he discovered a workshop or laboratory staffed and operated by a number of spider robots. Russell sensed that they were aware of his presence; but they ignored him and scuttled about their tasks with complete indifference. He stayed for a while, trying to find out what they were doing. But their actions and the equipment they were using made little sense to him.

Finally, when Anna called out anxiously, he went out into the sunlight and recounted what he had seen. It was only while he was trying to describe the interior to Farn zem Marur that Russell realized he had seen no source of light in the buildings, yet everything had been as visible as if the structures were made out of transparent glass, and the igloos were penetrated by daylight.

With time passing, the sun having passed its zenith, Russell became impatient to press on to the column and the green translucent bubble that rested on top of it, vast and awe-inspiring, yet still looking so insubstantial that it might drift away on the next breath of wind. But before they reached the column, they saw yet another group of buildings that were of an entirely different character from the previous ones. There were five of the buildings altogether, each made out of stone or concrete and shaped like a cone. The buildings were about thirty meters high, with small V-shaped openings in the walls near the bases. Russell crawled through one of the openings—it was not big enough for him to walk through—and found himself in semidarkness. When his eyes had adjusted to the gloom, he found that the building contained nothing but a series of plastic poles, each set horizontally in the wall, at right angles to it and parallel with the floor. If all the poles, each ten or twelve centimeters in diameter, had been extended, they would have met in the center of the building, like the spokes of a giant wheel whose rim was embedded in the walls. But each of the spokes was only four or five meters long. And there were many of them. Too many to be counted easily. . . .

They reminded him of something, but he could not recollect what it was until he was out in the sunlight once more, telling Anna and Farn zem Marur what he had seen.

Then he remembered. The poles reminded him of perches in a chicken house. And was it his imagination, or had there really been a trace of sweet-scented droppings on the floor of the gloomy interior? In retrospect, he felt that he had been oddly aware of recent occupation. But there was no evidence of this, and he dismissed it as a trick of the mind—suggested, perhaps, by his comparison of the poles with perches for fowls to roost upon.

Now, as the three of them stood at the base of the great metal column that rose giddily into the sky, supporting its green surrealistic bloom that cast a strange penumbra over the whole scene, Russell reviewed the events of the morning and was aware of two things. The first was that, apart from a brief glimpse of "fairies" or "demons," they had seen no living creatures. The second was that it was impossible to make any sense out of the evidence of civilization that had been discovered so far.

He was discouraged. He had lost his fear now and was simply discouraged. He did not know what he had really expected to find. Yet he had certainly not expected indifference and emptiness. He was beginning to think that they would have to go back to the boat without having discovered anything that would enable them to establish contact with their captors or that would explain some of the mystery of their predicament.

The column and the bubble were massive, silent, inscrutable. They might be nothing more, thought Russell bitterly, than some monstrous alien cenotaph. What a joke it would be if they had traveled this far only to find a vast memorial to the dead of an unknown race!

But what of the machines, the stores, the spider robots, the perches? His head was aching, and he was very tired. He looked at Anna and Farn zem Marur. The lines of fatigue and perplexity were etched on their faces, also.

"We are not winning," he said. "We are no wiser. Perhaps we ought to eat something, then get back to the boat before sunset if we can. By that time we shall all be in need of a good night's rest."

It was at that moment, as they turned away, that there was a great sound as of distant thunder.

Then a voice that seemed to fill the world rolled across the sky and spoke to them.

"Greetings!" it said. "From the Vruvyir to their children, greetings!"

Then, suddenly, all about them there was light and movement. And the air was a riot of iridescent wings.

28

The Vruvyir, Russell realized dimly, were not fairies, not demons, not dragonflies. They were *people*. They had supple, almost reptilian bodies with suckers in their tails, which they clamped firmly to the ground, their roost poles, or anything to which they wished to attach themselves. They had two pairs of short arms, two pairs of bright transparent wings, and dazzling golden tendrils which fell in shaggy profusion over their amber faces. And they had faces strangely like those of grave sea horses.

Yet they were people.

They were people because they had society and culture —and a science and a technology as yet undreamed of by such simple creatures as mankind. Above all, they were people because they had language—and the gift of tongues. Clearly, they were a great people.

Russell did not experience fear. He felt a great sensation of awe.

They had materialized—or so it seemed—out of thin air. And now they were ranged around the base of the great column, poised motionless upon their tails, occasionally fluttering their beautiful wings, and regarding with expressions of bland serenity the three human beings who confronted them.

Farn zem Marur stared at them with ashen face and with sword in hand. Anna held her crossbow unsteadily. Russell glanced at the grenade he was holding, then smiled and put it gently down at his feet.

The voice that seemed to fill the world rolled across the

sky and spoke to them again. Russell looked at the Vruvyir. Their faces were masklike, their sea horse lips immobile. Yet the voice that spoke impeccable English— and, he supposed, perfect Russian and perfect Gren Li— was a real voice. The sound of it seemed to shake the very earth on which he stood.

"The Vruvyir, having greeted their children, ask: Why have you come to this place?"

Russell licked his lips. The expressionless faces and the voice that came from nowhere unnerved him. When he spoke, his own voice was no more than a whisper. He could barely hear it himself, yet he was convinced that every one of the strange beings heard it clearly.

"Because there is much that we wish to know. Because we need to understand."

Laughter rolled across the sky. "Children! Children! You *need* to understand?"

"Yes, we need to understand," asserted Russell. "We need to know why we have been taken from our own worlds. We need to know why we were imprisoned behind a barrier of mist. We need to know what future there can be for us in a world that is not ours."

Again the laughter rolled. "Children! Does the rat in the cage need to understand the scientist's purpose? Does the earthworm need to grasp the ecology of nature? Does the amoeba need to comprehend parturition?"

Russell felt the tears stinging in his eyes and falling down his cheeks. Crazily, his mind was elsewhere. He was tormented by visions. He saw Absu mes Marur entering the bond. He saw Tore Norstedt building a boat. He saw Ireg giving him a stone ax. Were people such as these to be regarded as rats in a cage?

"We are not rats or worms or amoebas," he shouted. "Nor are we children. We are men and women. Compared

with such as you, we may have little knowledge or achievement. But we have pride, we have dignity, we have curiosity. We know what friendship is, and we are not without
some courage. You may destroy us, but you shall not defeat
us."

"Lord," murmured Farn zem Marur, "it is well spoken. I
am privileged to die in such company. Speak but the word,
and my sword shall answer."

"Russell," whispered Anna. "I am glad that we knew
each other. The journey was worthwhile."

Again the laughter rolled. "We are the Vruvyir. You are
our children—in whom we are well pleased."

Russell experienced a sudden blind rage. They, the
Vruvyir, were playing with their victims. Behind those
blank sea horse faces, he sensed silent laughter—profound
amusement, doubtless, at some great alien joke. He wanted
to smash something, to wipe the laughter out of their minds.
He looked at the grenade at his feet. He felt the lighter in
his pocket.

"So you are the master race!" he shouted. "So we are bar-
barians whom it amuses you to taunt! Well, we think the
joke is sour. We have a different sense of humor. Let us see
whether you will be amused."

He made a sign to Anna and Farn zem Marur. Then he
moved to pick up the grenade.

"Stay still!" thundered the voice. "Children, do not
destroy yourselves! You came here to understand. So be it.
But what if you cannot bear the burden of understanding?"

As the voice issued its command, Russell found that he
could not move his arms, his body, or his legs. It was as if
they had been set in invisible ice. With difficulty, he turned
his head—the only part of him that he could still move—
and looked at his companions. Farn and Anna also were
frozen into immobility. They had looks on their faces such

as he knew that he himself must be wearing. Looks in which incredulity and shock seemed to blend with a curious resignation.

He turned his head once more, with difficulty, and regarded the ranks of the Vruvyir. Even as he answered their question, he noted that there were not more than about fifty of these strange beings present. That was, somehow, important. There was something at the back of his mind that . . . He mentally shrugged the notion away as irrelevant.

"It is for us to decide if we can bear what you call the burden of understanding," he said calmly. "You may destroy us, as I have said. Indeed, it would seem that your task is an easy one, for we are few and you are many. Also, you have power such as we have never experienced. But while we are alive we exercise the right to think, the right to explore, the right to discover the real nature of our predicament."

"Brave words!" said the voice that filled the sky. "Proud words, spoken with the pride that is born of ignorance. The carnivore is supreme until it encounters the hunter, the hunter is supreme until he meets the warrior, the warrior is supreme until challenged by a greater warrior. Such is the pattern of life. . . . Little ones, you walk in the forest, yet you do not know the dangers of the forest. We, the Vruvyir, say this to you: knowledge can destroy, understanding can destroy. Do you still seek knowledge and understanding?"

Russell was silent for a moment or two. Then he said quietly, "We are familiar with destruction. We know that it is a part of life. . . . But it is better to be destroyed on strange frontiers than to live in a prison of ignorance and fear."

Again the laughter, but this time it was gentle. And

was there some new element in the eyes set boldly in those grave sea horse faces? Compassion?

Russell looked at them and was afraid.

The voice thundered on. "Children, little ones, hear that which, if at all, you will comprehend but dimly. . . . Think now of time. Not of personal time, for you are as the butterfly that lives a short space in a short season. Not of biological time, for life—simple life—is transient in its unfolding. Not of geological time, for even the existence of the rocks is as nothing to the burning of the stars. Think, then, of cosmic time. Think of the youth of the galaxy, of the great, gaseous whirls that ultimately became a thousand million suns. It was in such time, in the time that is no time, in the long, dusty dawn of galactic creation, that absolute life itself was born. . . . It did not begin in some primordial planetary ocean. It began as a thing of fire, born of the children of fire, incandescent with power, white hot with promise. . . . The stars are alive, little ones. And sometimes they dream. . . . And sometimes they give birth. . . .

"When the world you call the Earth was nothing, not even a swelling in the womb of a star that was too young to dream, there were already a million aging planets spawned by quicker, brighter fires. The original Vruvyir were not born on or of any such planets, little ones. Nor were they born of or in the normal scheme of time. They were born of a dying star, they coalesced from fire, they took form in vortices of pure energy. They were sentient firebirds, the product of direct stellar procreation. They danced, they lived, changing form constantly for the sheer joy of making new patterns. And in the end they leaped away from the parent star to pit themselves against the cold and the dark and the slow erosion of entropy that is the end of all things born of fire.

"They came to a planet, they endured, they starved themselves down to unimaginably low temperatures, they took permanent form, they learned the secrets of simple biological life. They, our ancestors, the great ones, deliberately froze themselves in the sluggish cycles of planetary existence, until they knew that the chosen form was sufficient for their self-appointed task. What was that task, little ones? They were to be no less than the source of low-temperature life."

The voice paused for a moment or two—long enough for Russell to realize that his head was aching, his mind was reeling, and his imagination was numbed. He glanced at Anna. Her face was haggard and drawn, her eyes wide and staring. He wanted to touch her, to comfort her. But he could not move. He wanted to fall down, even, but he could not move. He looked at Farn zem Marur, stiff and unseeing. And he was moved by a great pity. Farn zem Marur's medieval mind was already in retreat—perhaps soon to be followed by the more sophisticated minds of the two twentieth-century terrestrials.

Apparently unheeding, the great voice rolled on.

"The galaxy was a garden; the garden had yet to be planted. The Vruvyir carried the seed. They spread out between the fertile stars, some to fail in their task and to be destroyed by fire or darkness, some to bring movement and biological pattern to hitherto sterile worlds where the chemistry of life had yet to intrude upon the slow physics of stagnation.

"They came to a planet, little ones. Two thousand million years ago they came to the third planet of a mid-range star. They saw that the world was lifeless yet possessing great promise. So the Vruvyir came and they quickened the planet. They quickened it simply by defecating into the rich and vacant oceans. Such, children, was the origin of life on the planet you call Earth.

"The Vruvyir departed, the aeons passed. Then, less than a million Earth-years ago, they returned to this tiny corner of the garden. Great was their joy to find that life had flourished. Great was their interest to observe the life form destined to be dominant—an upright biped that used tools, that was learning the value of fire, and that was not afraid to dream.

"Samples were taken and distributed to worlds where the original quickening had yet to yield a form of such potential. Samples were taken and left to flourish. Now, on this world, samples of the original stock and also of the samples have been brought together, each in a familiar microcosm, so that the Vruvyir may observe their children and consider their destiny, and so that the children may discover one another. . . . And in such discovery fashion their own destiny. . . . For, as children will, each has flourished at a different pace and in a different way. For some the day of understanding has already dawned, while some still live in the predawn light. . . . Thus, the Vruvyir grant you the burden of knowledge. Make of it what you will."

There was silence.

There was a silence so profound that it seemed louder even than the voice that had rolled across the sky.

Russell looked at the ranks of the Vruvyir. Their wings remained still, their sea horse faces expressionless. There were not so many of them as he had at first thought—forty, perhaps. They looked many, but their numbers were few.

There was something at the back of his mind. Something important. If only he could think! If only his wits had not been bludgeoned into uselessness by such a fantastic encounter and such a fantastic revelation!

Then suddenly, irrationally, intuitively, Russell made the mental leap. The empty roosts, the silent city, the smallness and the greatness . . . All pointed to one mad conclusion.

He looked at Anna and Farn, exhausted with wonder, traumatized with knowledge. He thought of all his companions in the zoo—brought there and kept there because of the whim of the Vruvyir, the master race, the source of life, the lords of the galaxy.

And he took the gamble.

It was a crazy thought. But then, was anything sane in a nightmare such as this? Surely only the unreasonable could be reasonable? Only the absurd could have any bearing on reality.

He spoke.

"You have called us your children. And, if there is truth in what you have said—and, strange though it may be, there is the ring of truth—you must realize that children sometimes stumble on the answer to a question that has not been asked."

Again the laughter. Again the voice that filled the sky.

"What, then, is the answer to this question that has not been asked?"

Russell gazed at the expressionless faces that confronted him.

And took a deep breath. "You brought us—the samples, as you call us—together because there is little time left. We have seen your city. It is a city of ghosts. . . . The Vruvyir are dying."

It was a crazy thought, prompted by many things—the lack of previous contact, the number of poles in the "chicken roost," the sense of emptiness that seemed to pervade the entire landscape surrounding the city. . . .

Laughter seemed to shake the firmament.

Again there was the voice of the Vruvyir, the voice of the world.

"A valiant guess, little one. A proposition of some interest—but wrong. The Vruvyir are not dying. They are already dead."

29

"Look up, children," continued the voice. "Look up at the last Sphere of Creation in the known worlds. It is beautiful, is it not?"

Russell's mind was reeling. He was no longer aware of Anna and Farn zem Marur. They might never have existed —except perhaps as phantoms in some half-forgotten dream. He was alone in a world of aliens. He was alone with sea horses, fairies, demons, dragonflies, and the secret of the ages. He knew that he was on the verge of madness, and the knowledge made him unnaturally calm. It was as if someone had poured iced water into his brain. As if someone—or something—had taken control of volition, emotion, reasoning, acceptance, credulity. As if someone —or something—were holding him in case he should fall.

He looked up the great column—smooth, hypnotic, awe-inspiring, beautiful. He looked up the great column at the green translucent bubble, the Sphere of Creation that seemed now to cast its green penumbra over the entire world.

"It is beautiful," whispered Russell, unaware even of his whispering. "It is surely the most beautiful thing there is."

"It is the last of the great machines," went on the voice, "the last refuge of the Vruvyir. When the kinetic fails, the ghosts of the ghosts will fail, one by one, and the Vruvyir will live only in those who come after. . . . Be afraid, little ones, but not too much afraid. The burden of knowledge is heavy."

Russell tried desperately to marshal his tumbling

thoughts. "You say the Vruvyir are dead. Yet we have seen them—or what is left of them. They—you—are here, speaking to us, telling us the strangest of all the stories of creation. You are presuming to be gods, yet you also say that the gods are dead."

The laughter—touched now, so Russell thought, with an immense sadness—rolled once more.

"Little one, we are ghosts speaking to ghosts. Thus far you have come. There is a little farther to go. The price you must pay is measured in biological time. Are you willing to pay such a price?"

"We wish to know," said Russell, almost hysterically. "We wish to know. We have endured much, we have risked death to discover why we are here and what you, our jailers, are like. . . . We wish to know! How did we come here? Why do you say that we are ghosts also?"

"Children, you have presumed. But your presumption is interesting. The answers you seek lie in the Sphere of Creation. Find them, and be content."

Suddenly, momentarily, the world became dark.

Then the darkness lifted.

It lifted upon a soft green light. It lifted upon a soft green hum of energy. It lifted in the Sphere of Creation.

Russell was falling or drifting or swimming. He had no sense of direction, no sense of time, and little sense of identity. He was in a green ocean or a green cloud or a green void. He did not know whether he was alone or not alone. He knew only that he existed.

He could not see himself—his hands, his arms, his body. He could not see his companions. He knew only that he existed.

The greenness deepened.

It became a blueness.

The blueness deepened.

It became a blackness.

And there were stars—known stars. The constellations seen from Earth.

And then the constellations were blotted out as a great discus—black in shadow, blinding in sunlight—swung silently out of the void.

He was inside the discus, and it was not a discus but some tremendous vehicle of space, cavernous, complex, alien. He was in a chamber where strange machinery seemed to produce a muted, melancholy throb of music. He was in a chamber where spider robots scuttled about their tasks oblivious of his invisible and insubstantial presence.

Suddenly part of the floor of the chamber turned to glass—or so it seemed. There, spread out below, still and colorful as a contour map, lay northern Europe, the North Sea, and the islands of Britain.

The discus fell like a stone. The North Sea zoomed up to swallow it. Then instantly, without shock or vibration, the fantastic fall was annihilated. Beneath the transparent floor, a hundred meters below, a passenger aircraft hung as if suspended from the discus by invisible wires.

The sea moved. The jet seemed motionless. Velocities had been matched.

The transparent floor rolled noiselessly away. The spider robots hauled a mounted tube, oddly like a small astronomical telescope, into position. The tube was depressed on its mounting until it was aligned with the aircraft.

He recognized the aircraft.

The passenger jet from Stockholm to London.

A green radiance, a bar of radiance that seemed as solid as a rod of crystal, shot down to the aircraft, danced about it, englobed it.

The Stockholm to London jet was caught in a green bubble.

The bubble grew, shimmered and grew. The sphere became an egg. The egg developed a waist. The waist narrowed. And then there were two bubbles, translucent, touching, one poised on top of the other. Alien soap bubbles blown above the world of man.

In the lower bubble the aircraft was held frozen, captive.

In the top bubble there was . . . there was a vortex of light, a whirlpool of energy, a dervish dance of shadows, a ripple of condensing outlines, a shiver of forms, a freeze of patterns.

An act of recreation.

And now there were two identical aircraft locked in great green bubbles. And now the spider robots, with the exhausts from jet attachments on their pseudolimbs writing brief vapor messages in the sky, drifted lazily down and into the top bubble, coming to rest upon the skin of the duplicate aircraft. And after them, like surrealist sausages, drifted a string of sixteen green plastic containers. Man-sized.

The spider robots opened the door into the plane. Two of them entered it. Presently they began to hand out life-size dolls, stiff, immobile. The dolls were laid carefully into the containers. The lids were closed. The containers, each nursed by a spider robot, were lifted out of the green bubble and brought up to the great discus that hung over the world.

Presently sixteen containers and sixteen spider robots had entered the discus. Presently the top bubble popped, exploded, imploded, disappeared. And there was no duplicate aircraft. Nothing.

Presently the lower bubble popped silently.

And the jet from Stockholm to London continued unconcernedly on its way.

The opening in the great space vehicle closed, and it rose toward the stars.

Then the stars dissolved, and Russell was lost once more in the green void of the Sphere of Creation. He was neither living nor dead. . . . He was no more than a green thought in a green shade—a thread of consciousness in the profound, impossible silence of unbeing.

The thread shivered, and the movement became clothed in whispers. . . .

"Thus do ghosts create ghosts. Thus were the facsimiles obtained. As it was with the aircraft traveling from Stockholm to London, so also was it with the red spice caravan journeying from the Kingdom of Ullos to the Upper and Lower Kingdoms of Gren Li. So, too, with the settlement of those you call the People of the River. They, like you and your companions, were englobed by projected Spheres of Creation. The replicas were made, though the originals were unaware of their manufacture. The replicas were made—molecule for molecule, heartbeat for heartbeat, thought for thought. . . . Thus Russell Grahame, Member of Parliament for Middleport North, has returned to London and has resigned from the Parliamentary Labour Party. Thus Anna Markova, privileged now and then to journey from Moscow to Western Europe, continues to write her features for the Russian press. Thus Farn zem Marur serves Absu mes Marur, gonfalonier of the western keeps, in a far country and in the name of the white queen and the black. . . .

"The burden of knowledge is heavy, is it not?" went on the whispering voice. "Little one, how will you face the realization that you and your companions are no more than replicas of those who knew not that the very pattern of their bodies and minds would be infused into an alien world? Russell Grahame is elsewhere. Anna Markova is elsewhere. Farn zem Marur is elsewhere. All who live behind the barrier of mist are duplicates of those who exist elsewhere. Duplicates with slight modification of the language areas. Duplicates supplied with duplicate foods, duplicate animals, duplicate habitations. Have the Vruvyir then abducted you from your own world? Demonstrably, they have not. They created you. Surely you are their property?"

There was silence. A green silence. Time was demolished. Minutes, hours, days, years, centuries drowned in the opaque green ocean that existed in the Sphere of Creation. The being who had thought of himself as Russell Grahame almost drowned with them.

But somewhere . . . somewhere there was a cry of defiance, a courageous rearguard action of sanity, a surge of affirmation.

"I am!" shouted a disembodied voice. "I am myself! I exist! I think! I sorrow! I hope! I am no one's property! I am a man!"

Came the whisper once more. "Little one, is it greatness or is it madness? You have seen what you have seen."

"I am myself!" shouted the voice. "Let who can destroy me! None shall possess me!"

"Child," said the whisper, "truly you are alive. That much you may know. You are alive and with the ability to create new life. And in this you are greater than those who crossed the light-years to fashion you in the image of a man. The Vruvyir are dead. They have played their part since the dawn of creation. But now they are dead. You are the living, creative image of a man. They are no more than ghosts of ghosts, duplicated as you were—but not from the image itself, only from the image of an image of an image through unimaginable epochs. They reach to you from the past. Their greatness and their skills are almost spent. You and your kind—their children indeed—are an act of faith, an offering to the future. . . . Child, tomorrow, or the day after, or the year after, or the century or the millennium after, the mnemonic will fail, the kinetic will fail, and the last Sphere of Creation will be no more than a legend in the minds of children. Let the children of your children's children live to demonstrate that the Vruvyir, leaping from their parent star, did not leap in vain. . . . Rest now, for the burden is heavy. Rest now, and prepare to pay the price for reaching out into the deeps."

The greenness rippled, became deeper. There was nothing in all eternity but the drunkenness of an absolute fatigue. There was nothing in all eternity but the blackness of oblivion.

30

Daylight crept up over the edge of the great green savanna to reveal two plastic coffins/boxes lying in the middle of the road between the hotel and the supermarket. A Stone Age warrior, incongruously wearing a jacket of animal skins, tattered woven trousers, and plaited sandals, with a *steel* ax in his hand and half a dozen plucked chickens held by their extended necks and slung loosely over his shoulder, walked purposefully out of the green wilderness and along the strip of road toward the Erewhon Hilton.

He saw the coffins and stopped.

He saw the coffins just as their occupants pushed the lids off.

Russell was the first to climb out. He gazed around him, blinked, staggered a little, then held his head. Then he heard Anna groan, lying by his feet. He stooped and helped her up. They held each other tightly for a moment, saying nothing—because there was too much to say.

They gazed wonderingly at the silent hotel. Then they noticed the Stone Age warrior.

With a great shout he dropped ax and chickens and ran toward them. Even as he moved, there was an answering shout from the Erwhon Hilton.

"Russell, my friend!" said Ireg. "Anna! It has been a long time. You live. That is enough. My heart is very full." He hugged them both.

Russell and Anna stared at him, stupefied. When they

had last talked with him, Ireg's vocabulary had been
limited to that of a very primitive savage.

"How long?" demanded Russell intently.

Ireg grinned broadly. "Long enough for me to learn
much. My head hurts with all that learning."

Before Russell could get him to amplify the statement,
people began to pour out of the Erewhon Hilton. Familiar
faces. Familiar voices. And yet . . .

And yet there was the difference.

They were leaner and tougher. Their skins were crinkled
and cracked with sunlight and wind. Their bodies were
hard with exertion and straight with confidence.

But the big difference was age.

John Howard's hair was a silvered gray. Marion Redman
was heavily pregnant. Robert Hyman had lost an arm, and
the stump was healed. Selene Bergere carried a baby at her
breast. Mohan das Gupta was blind. And there were
changes, subtle changes, in the others.

Russell licked his lips. He looked at Anna. She was sway-
ing. He put out his arm to steady her.

People were talking, laughing, crying, asking questions.
He heard nothing but the thought that rolled like thunder
in his head: "Surely it was only the day before yesterday
. . . only the day before yesterday."

He looked at John Howard, saw that his lips were moving, and could not concentrate upon the words. Before
the explanations, before the handshaking and the kissing,
there was that terrible, urgent question.

Russell looked at John Howard and cut across the flow
of words.

"How long? How long is it, John?"

The babel stopped.

"Long enough," he answered, gently. "Quite long
enough. . . . We thought you were dead."

"How bloody long?"

"Take it easy, Russell. . . . You don't know?"

"God dammit, I'm asking you!"

"Three and a half years—our time." John Howard smiled. "Now, how long has it been in your time?"

But Russell was too busy catching Anna as she fainted.

At the same time, John was recovering from his own sense of shock. "Come on, everybody," he snapped briskly. "Let's get them inside and give them both a chance to pull around. We'll all find out what has been happening, soon enough. And let's move those bloody boxes out of the way. They bring back too many memories."

Presently Russell and Anna were leaning back in two of the comfortable chairs in the lounge of the Erewhon Hilton. Anna had only fainted momentarily. The color was now coming back into her cheeks as she slowly sipped a glass of water.

John had banished everyone from the room except Ireg and Marion Redman, who as time passed had come to be regarded as the group's official doctor. He had wanted to banish Ireg, also; but Ireg had turned a deaf ear to his plea. Were not Russell and Anna his friends? Had he not been the first to find them? John Howard did not press his argument too strongly with over two hundred pounds of partly educated Stone Age warrior.

Marion said, "Feeling better now? It's bad enough to be brought here once in a box—but to be brought here twice . . ." She gazed at the pair of them compassionately.

"I am all right," said Anna. "It was stupid of me. I am all right now. It was just that—" Words failed her. Russell held her hand tightly.

"There's no hurry," said John. "No hurry at all. Would you like me to give a potted version of our side of the story? Then, when you are ready, you can tell us a little of what has happened to you. And we can fill in all the details later."

Russell took a deep breath. "We'd like that very much." He smiled. "But just to ensure that the amazement is not too one-sided, I think you ought to know that we are only aware of being away for about a couple of days."

John gazed at him open-mouthed. Russell suddenly felt much better. "Have a glass of water," he suggested. "You look as if you need it."

"Touché," said John. "Shocks for all. I'll try to contain myself until you have heard our bit. . . . About ten days after you went sailing bravely off in that little boat, we began to have serious doubts. After about a month most of us were convinced that you had all had it. . . . Where is Farn, by the way? Is he alive?"

Russell and Anna looked at each other blankly. After a moment Russell said, "We don't know. I'm betting he has been delivered by express parcel to Keep Marur much in the same way as we were brought here. . . . I hope he's alive; but in a little while I'll tell you all that happened—or all that we *think* happened. It is still your turn."

"Sorry. Where was I? Yes, by that time we thought you were dead. We mourned you; but life has to go on. We had to do something, we had to make plans—if only to stop us all going neurotic. But one thing our plans did not include was another attempt at passing through the mist barrier. At least, not until we knew more and not until we were better equipped. . . . So we decided to educate and consolidate. Not only ourselves," he glanced at Ireg, "but any other human beings in the same predicament. We felt we had to find some basis for understanding and accepting each other. It seemed a useful task."

"It's much more than that," said Russell grimly. "It is our only hope of survival and sanity."

"You recollect that Janice started to rear chickens?" asked John.

Russell smiled. "As if it were yesterday."

"We didn't know it at the time, but it turned out to be terribly important. It brought about a social and historical revolution."

Anna joined in. "Chickens do not cause revolutions," she observed tartly. "People are needed—special people."

"In this case, both were needed," said John. "Within three years our Stone Age friends"—he turned to Ireg— "you don't mind us calling you Stone Age People?"

"Not at all, John." Ireg grinned. "We call you the Canned Food People."

"Well said, Ireg, old friend." Russell began to laugh.

"Within three years," went on John, "Ireg and his friends have become highly successful poultry farmers. It has changed their attitudes and their entire economy. They have found a local substitute for wheat—it's one of those high, tough grasses. The seeds taste like sweet corn dipped in vinegar. They have also discovered a kind of wild cabbage and something that looks and tastes like a cross between potato and onion. In short, they have switched to an agrarian culture."

"And how did all that come about?"

"Janice—a woman to whom I take off my hat—went to live with them. Ireg and Ora came to visit us fairly frequently, and after a time she went back with them, taking a dozen hens and a cock. Originally it was just to show them how to cope with the hens and get eggs and chickens. She stayed in the River Settlement for a fortnight or so. Then she came back here for a while. But she couldn't settle. She had found a mission in life. So she went back to the River Settlement, and she has been there ever since.

She has been teaching farming to the men and domestic science to the women. Now—God save us—she is teaching them to read and write."

"A B C D E F G," said Ireg complacently, "H I J K L M N O P, Q R S T U V W X Y Z. Once two is two, two twos are four, three twos are six, four twos are eight, five twos are ten. I have ten fingers and ten toes, and that makes twenty. What do you think of that, Russell?"

"I think," said Russell gravely, "that you are a great man, Ireg." He turned to John once more. "What about our friends at Keep Marur?"

John grinned. "They are tougher nuts to crack than the Stone Age People. The trouble is that they have some sophistication and some learning, but they also have a hell of a lot of rigid orthodoxy. Absu can't get it into his head that we are not magicians. It does not, thank goodness, stop him from cooperating in important ventures. But he still thinks we do it all by mirrors."

"What kind of important ventures?"

"Number one project is the building of a glider."

"A glider?" Anna was nonplussed.

"A man-carrying glider," said John. "We thought you were dead. We thought you had frozen in the mist barrier. So, we reasoned, if we can't pass through the mist, we shall have to pass over it. There are plenty of good thermals in this big prison of ours. Pulpul hide, incidentally, is much stronger and lighter than plywood, when it is cured properly. We demonstrated the principle of heavier-than-air machines to Absu with small models. So now we are working together on the construction of a light two-man glider. It should be ready in a month or two."

"How will you launch it?"

"Teams of pulpuls. They run pretty fast when required."

There was a brief silence. Russell's head was reeling.

There were so many more questions he wanted to ask, so much he wanted to say.

"Look here," said John, eyeing them both. "There is such a lot to tell you that it will take days. We are, as you have already seen, well into the second generation. We've had accidents—Robert losing an arm felling timber and Mohan trying to blow himself to glory with explosives—but we'll give you the domestic score when you have rested, and when we have had your own news."

Russell sighed. So much had happened in the time they had lost. But then, also, so much had happened in the time they had known. So much that was frightening. And wonderful.

There was the echo of a whisper in his head: "The burden of knowledge is heavy, is it not?" The burden was indeed heavy—the burden of being a carbon copy. Was it right to share such a burden, and in so doing, perhaps, erode in his friends the sense of individuality that was so important for survival? Neither he nor Anna had yet been able to truly assimilate or accept what they had learned. They were both still in a state of shock. Perhaps in the end it would not matter to either of them that Anna Markova, Mark One, was somewhere in Europe scribbling away at her trade, or that Russell Grahame, Mark One, had retired from politics and was either drinking himself to death in the provinces or making a pile in industry.

He looked at her, perplexed. He looked at her with a question in his eyes. Anna looked back and smiled. The answer was in her eyes. Intuitively, he knew it was the right answer. Intuitively, he knew that he could accept neither the responsibility nor the right to keep such knowledge to himself.

Russell spoke to Ireg first. "Ireg, my friend, forgive me. I am asking you to leave us now. What I have to say is hard to tell even to my own people. Someday I will tell it to you. But just now the thoughts are too big for me to find the right words."

Ireg left with dignity. "Russell, it is good that you come back to us. I—I understand. Janice calls us her children, and I know that there are things children cannot know. We will talk soon?"

"We will talk soon."

Somewhat self-consciously, Ireg shook Russell's hand.

When he had gone, Marion said: "You are sure you want to tell us about it now? You both look pretty shattered to me."

"I had better tell you about it now," said Russell. "Later may be too late, because already I am almost beginning to doubt what has happened. . . . One question before I start. Have you had any more encounters with the 'fairies'?"

"We have seen them, but not recently," said John. "And always they are in flight. And always they disappear as soon as someone notices them."

"They have faces like sea horses," said Russell.

"Sea horses?"

"Very solemn sea horses."

"What kind of creatures are they?"

"Ghosts. They are our masters. But they are only ghosts of ghosts."

John Howard took a deep breath. "Why not begin at the beginning?"

"Why not, indeed?" said Russell. "And the beginning was the mist barrier."

As he talked, his fatigue seemed to fall away. He knew that he would pay for it later. But as he talked, he was aware of a new sensation. Compassion. Compassion for the Vruvyir—for the doomed master race that had leaped out among the stars to disseminate life and to pay for it with their own mortality. He felt he was beginning to understand the Vruvyir. He felt he was beginning to hear their music. Or was it all an illusion? Because, after all, they were now no more than ghosts.

He told John and Marion of the experience of passing through the mist barrier. He described his first glimpse of the great column and of the green translucent bubble that was the Sphere of Creation. He told of the encounter with the spider robots and of the journey to the city that was itself a complex mausoleum. Then he tried to describe the appearance/materialization/projection of the Vruvyir. And finally, stumbling over his own words, seeking and failing to find the right nuance, the appropriate image, he tried to convey some impression of his own experience in the Sphere of Creation.

When he had finished, Russell was exhausted. When he had finished, John and Marion were dumbfounded. When he had finished, Anna was weeping.

Presently, John said: "So we too are ghosts?"

"Living ghosts," retorted Russell. "*Doppelgängers* with the ability to procreate. We can breed reality. The Vruvyir cannot. They can duplicate, but they cannot breed. Their energies are spent."

"And you say the original Vruvyir created life on Earth and that they then seeded other planets?"

"So we were led to believe." Russell shrugged. "I'm not asking you to believe *us*, John. I'm merely reporting in my own garbled fashion what passed between us and the Vruvyir and what I, at least, experienced in the Sphere of Creation."

"My experience was pretty much the same as Russell's," said Anna. "It was totally subjective. It might just be an hallucination. But for me it was real."

John Howard sighed. "Much as it goes against my

scientific training, I believe you both. I believe what you say, and I even believe what the Vruvyir said or revealed to you. I believe it because it is fantastic." He laughed grimly. "If you had given me a tolerably rational explanation of our circumstances, I probably would not have accepted a word of it."

"What do they want of us?" said Marion suddenly. "What do these terrible creatures want of us?"

"There is a phrase that seems to be etched in my mind," said Russell quietly. " 'Let the children of your children's children live to demonstrate that the Vruvyir, leaping from their parent star, did not leap in vain.' "

"On Earth," said Anna suddenly, "on Earth there are enough nuclear weapons to annihilate mankind about seventeen times. Perhaps the Vruvyir can predict the end of such a buildup. Perhaps they want to salvage something —if it is worth salvaging. . . . Perhaps they want us to grow."

John wrinkled his forehead and ran a hand through the gray hair. "So we and Sept Marur and the Stone Age People are of one blood?"

"We always were," said Russell enigmatically, "in case you hadn't noticed."

"What of the future?"

"It belongs to us—not to the Vruvyir. . . . It seems we are here to stay—to live or die. Some day there will be no more Vruvyir. Some day, I believe, there will be no mist barrier, no groceries delivered by obliging metal spiders. We shall be on our own. We are the inheritors."

"So what do we do? Build a new society? Integrate? Utopia on Erewhon?" He laughed bitterly. "And the classic question: Would you want your daughter to marry a Stone Age savage?"

Russell was tired. "There is the classic answer. I would

only want my daughter to marry a man. . . . Let's make
the best of it, John. We can do no more."

"They are going to rest now," said Marion with deter-
mination. "They have been pushed to the limit, and they
are going to rest. We have all the time in the world to talk
about these things. Now they need a bit of peace."

Even while she was speaking, Anna had closed her eyes.
Russell put his hand on her breast, then closed his eyes,
also. They slept through most of the day.

That evening, just before sunset, Absu mes Marur rode to
the Erewhon Hilton. He was surprised to find Anna and
Russell apparently in their right minds.

"Farn zem Marur, pathfinder and warrior of some
talent, also has returned to his sept," said Absu. Then he
added inscrutably, "Therefore, I rejoice to find my friends as
they are."

"How is Farn?" asked Russell. "Is he well and rested?"

Absu met the question with another question. "Lord
Russell," said Absu formally, "I require to know how my
pathfinder bore himself. Did he bring dishonor to his sept?"

Russell was shaken. "Farn zem Marur, your servant and
our friend and companion, is a brave man. He endured
much and with great courage."

"Then there is no debt to pay?"

Russell was puzzled. "What kind of debt?"

Absu appeared tremendously relieved. "No matter, Russell. It was my duty to ask. I am glad the pathfinder carried
himself as a man. That is enough."

"How is he?"

"Dead."

"Dead!"

"He returned," said Absu, "tormented by visions. He
spoke of a green sun and of voices and of dragons. He
spoke much that I could neither understand nor wish to

understand. Finally, realizing his own affliction in a moment of lucidity, he ran upon a lance. Perhaps it was best. I did not care to look upon him in such distress."

"Absu," said Russell, "Farn zem Marur was not mad. He was a valiant comrade, and I do not doubt that he spoke truly of what he had seen and heard. It is hard for me to find the words to tell you, but I will try to explain all that happened to us."

When he had finished speaking, Absu remained silent. He was silent for a long time. He, Russell, and Anna were sitting by themselves on the steps outside the hotel, watching the stars turn bleakly and remotely in a still strange and alien sky.

"Clearly," said Absu at length, "the Vruvyir are great magicians." He smiled. "But you also are a sept of magicians. Therefore the odds are not too great."

Russell shook his head. "There is no war, Absu. It is not a question of lances or of magic."

"I know that, my friend. We have a task. It is our task to demonstrate that we are men."

"It is our task," said Anna, "to show that we are one race."

"Above all," said Russell simply, "we have to grow. We really have to grow."

But it was Absu mes Marur, duplicate of Absu mes Marur, lord of sept Marur, gonfalonier of the western keeps, and charioteer of the red spice caravans, who summed it all up. "It is written," he said softly, "that if the seed be fertile, and if the weather be passing fair, the harvest will be bountiful. It is written in the earth. It is written in the sky."

EPILOGUE

In the year 741 A.V. at Port Grahame, the first orbital rocket sat on its launching pad. The skin was of pyrotitanium; and upon it, painted in deep crimson, there was the emblem of a sea horse with wings.

Two kilometers away in a blockhouse that had been built on the site of a hotel demolished long ago, a man and a woman watched the countdown.

Jansel Guptiregson had long golden hair and a deceptively beautiful face that concealed the mind of a brilliant mathematician. Varn Graymark was bald and small and intensely masculine. He was the telecommunications expert. They loved each other. But then, they loved many people.

"Ninety seconds," said Varn. "All systems operate. What can stop us now? That damned old sea horse is going to lift."

"There is no such creature as a sea horse, Varn. I don't know why you insisted on the symbol. Why not a winged pulpul? Why not a flying lance?"

"You've read the Book of Howard?"

"Sixty seconds. Of course I've read the Book of Howard. It is still required in middle school. Though why they can't give a bit more time to comparative religion, I'll never know."

"In the Book of Howard," said Varn, "there is the story of creation. You will recall, no doubt, the Lord Russell's encounter with the winged sea horse in the Globe of Life."

"So?"

"So I like the notion. It's absurd, beautiful. I like it. . . . Forty-five seconds."

"But why a myth? Why not something real? Something practical?"

Varn Graymark laughed. "You, a mathematician, deriding myths! What will I hear next?"

"Thirty seconds," said Jansel. "Myth or not, it is a beautiful creature. I suppose it is the kind of nonsense that appeals."

Varn laughed. "My mother still believes that Lord Russell was the first man to break out of the Garden of Erewhon. She prays to his ghost every night."

"Do you believe in ghosts?"

"Twenty seconds. No, I believe in people. But one should always be able to afford some spiritual extravagance."

"Fifteen seconds," said Jansel. "What is your spiritual extravagance?"

Varn Graymark laughed. "I want to find a place that doesn't exist," he said. "That's why I was drawn to rocketry. I want to find a planet called Earth. The abode of the gods."

"Ten," said Jansel. "You're crazy."

"Nine. So I am."

"Eight. I want your child."

"Seven. It's a pleasure."

"Six. What shall we call him?"

"Five. Absu."

"Four. Why?"

"Three. Because."

"Two. Unanswerable."

"One. You understand."

"Zero. I understand."

"It's away!" shouted Varn exuberantly. "It's up and

away! The first stage in the journey. A fiery sea horse leaping out among the stars."

He peered through the triple window, listening to the muted roar of the rocket engines. It sounded like a great chord of music swelling to the sky. For a moment the crimson sea horse seemed to sit majestically on a tail of fire. Then, as if having made a decision, it rose, accelerating smoothly through the long arc that led to an orbital path.

Varn Graymark was thinking; and as usual, he was thinking fancifully. This day a key was turning in a lock. This day a door would be opened. This day a staircase would be revealed.

No doubt it would be a long and hazardous climb to the stars. But surely it was in the very nature of man to make such journeys. Just as it was in the nature of man to dream such dreams.